New Series
ROMANTIC COMEDY

Whoever you are, don't screw up now!

Strong hands settled on Ivy's shoulders and she sighed, trying to convince herself that she'd been lying here half-asleep and defenseless. If some strange man kissed her and she…didn't hate it…and decided to go to bed with him, she wouldn't feel guilty. She hadn't started this; her unfaithful husband had.

So she kept her eyes closed, let her body go limp and receptive and resorted to telepathy. A warm, firm mouth touched the corner of hers…and then he placed a kiss full on her mouth, his tongue nudging her lips apart insistently while one hand moved smoothly to cover her breast—

So much for fantasy. She sat up abruptly.

"Dammit!" She gave him a shove that landed her husband on his butt with a soft grunt of surprised protest. "I'd know that kiss anywhere, Jack Conrad!"

Dear Reader,

With the seasons changing and thoughts of winter not so far off, what better way to keep up our spirits than with a good dose of love and laughter?

This month we are thrilled to offer two charming and wonderful books written by two very popular authors. Vicki Lewis Thompson is a regular contributor to Harlequin Temptation and Superromance. Her light and lively style makes her a natural for writing LOVE & LAUGHTER, and her story about a pair of unlikely lovers trapped together is filled with tension and humor—and a truly wacky neighbor. I think we can all relate to the heroine's predicament: meeting an absolutely gorgeous guy while stuck in a doggy door!

Ruth Jean Dale continues to be a writing sensation. She launched her career in Temptation but then quickly branched out into Harlequin Romance, Superromance and Historical. *The Seven-Year Itch* is funny and romantic, a treat to read. Ivy's attempted revenge on her husband's *supposed* infidelity backfires in the most delightful ways....

With love—and laughter,

Malle Vallik

Malle Vallik
Associate Senior Editor

THE SEVEN-YEAR ITCH
Ruth Jean Dale

Harlequin Books

TORONTO • NEW YORK • LONDON
AMSTERDAM • PARIS • SYDNEY • HAMBURG
STOCKHOLM • ATHENS • TOKYO • MILAN
MADRID • WARSAW • BUDAPEST • AUCKLAND

ISBN 0-373-44006-5

THE SEVEN-YEAR ITCH

Copyright © 1996 by Betty Duran

Printed in U.S.A.

Be funny, my editor said.

Yeah, right. Me, be funny? I've never been funny in my life...not deliberately, anyway. In fact, when people suggest that I am, I usually ask if they mean funny ha-ha or funny weird. I admit I do see the humor in most situations, but I don't think of myself as funny. I don't even tell jokes, because I can't remember them. Well, I do have one, embedded in my brain years ago by my young daughter. Here, such as it is, is my only joke.

Question: What do you get when you pour boiling water down a rabbit hole? *Answer:* Hot cross bunnies!

Hey, *I* laughed.

I will, however, modestly confess to having what is often called "a good sense of humor"—that dreaded attribute given in our youth, usually by our mothers, to girls without other more obvious attributes. I'll find a way to laugh at just about anything, including catastrophes that would incapacitate more lugubrious souls.

And then I tell the world about near disasters such as the brain aneurysm that nearly did me in a decade ago. That's funny? I thought so when I wrote *One More Chance,* a Harlequin Temptation novel that makes me laugh just thinking about it.

Real life. That's where I find humor. If I didn't laugh, I'd cry, and I don't like to cry. When I get deep into a project such as *The Seven-Year Itch* I literally laugh myself silly in front of my computer screen.

Is that *funny weird* or *funny ha-ha?*

I think I'd better talk to my editor again....

—Ruth Jean Dale

1

"IVY EILEEN CONRAD, what have you been up to? If I've ever seen a guilty expression, you're wearing it."

Ivy snapped upright from a close examination of her flushed face in the subtly lighted mirror of the plush ladies' room in the Florida country club. "I—why, I've—I'm not—" She stopped short, realizing she was verifying her mother's observation with every word that tumbled from her mouth. Taking a deep breath, she said, "Nothing!"

"Ri-i-i-ight." Joan Jensen leaned heavily on the crutch wedged under her left arm. The plaster-cast-encased toes of one foot peeked out beneath the long full skirt of her jersey dress, which was the exact color of her carefully beige hair. Raising her brows, she rolled her eyes in mock endorsement of her daughter's prevarication. "Ivy, dear," she coaxed, "this is your mother talking. You can tell *me*."

As if! "There's nothing to tell," Ivy said firmly. Actually, there was, but she knew from experience that when the subject was temptation, her mother would be of little, if any, help. Opening her small black evening bag, Ivy extracted a shiny tube of lipstick and uncapped it, managing to whack off a crimson chunk in the process.

Joan lowered herself onto a blue brocade ottoman. "Okay, I'll figure it out on my own," she announced.

"I'll reconstruct the evening. You seemed to be having a good time earlier...."

"I'm still having a good time." Ivy slammed the golden tube back together, nicking off another waxy red blob. Stifling an exclamation not meant for a mother's ears, she snatched a tissue from a wall dispenser and set about cleaning up what was left of her favorite lipstick.

"Sure you are." Joan's face bore a look of calculation. "Let's consider the facts. You were just fine when Martin picked us up."

"I'm still just fine."

"You seemed to enjoy dinner."

"Dinner was wonderful. We just don't get fish like that in Dallas." Ivy edged toward the door, hoping to forestall further comment. "Don't you think we should be getting back? Martin will be wonder—"

"In a moment, dear." Joan eased her cast into a more comfortable position while regarding her daughter with a frown. "Have we been boring you?" she asked suddenly. "Is that it?"

"Mother! Don't be silly."

"I've tried to introduce you to all the nicest young people. Of course, I'd already told everyone so much about my beautiful daughter that—"

"Your *married* daughter."

"Of course." How could the mother of a thirty-one-year-old look so guileless? "Who could forget dear Jake?"

"That's *Jack* and you know it." Ivy gripped her purse so tightly that she felt an acrylic fingernail snap. "Good Lord, Mother, I've been married for almost seven years—in fact, it'll be seven years next month."

"On Valentine's Day," Joan said, rolling her eyes. "Wasn't that a little hokey, dear?"

"It was romantic," Ivy said firmly. "Under the circumstances, it looks like you could remember my husband's name."

"Jake, Jack, Jock, Jerk, what's the difference." Joan waved aside inconsequential details. "You're just trying to change the subject."

"I'm doing no such—"

"Here you are at last." Joan's friend Trudy bustled through the arched entryway, preceded by her voice. "And Ivy, too. I was beginning to think you'd both got lost."

"Well, we didn't," Joan said. "We're just having a nice little mother-daughter chat. Ivy was about to tell me what she—"

"Nothing, Mother. I have nothing to tell you." Ivy smiled brightly at Trudy. "I'll just run along and let the two of you talk."

"But, Ivy!"

"Now, Mother—"

Trudy patted Ivy's elbow. "Yes, you run along, dear. Don't keep Bart waiting."

"Bart!" Joan half rose from her position on the ottoman, lost her balance and fell back with an exclamation of surprise. "Bart Van Horn? Land developer Bart Van Horn? *Handsome* land developer Bart Van Horn? Oh, Ivy, why didn't you tell me?"

Because, Ivy thought, waving off her mother and making for the door, *you can't even remember your son-in-law's name.*

And because a few minutes ago, I was kind of having a problem with that myself.

HANDSOME, RICH land developer Bart Van Horn was indeed waiting for Ivy outside the ladies' room door. "Now, Bart—" she began in a warning tone.

He lifted his hands in a gesture of appeal, giving her a charming smile. "An honest mistake," he said with good cheer. "I had no idea you were married, Ivy. Now that I do..." His shrug could mean anything from "I won't do it again" to "I'll be more subtle next time."

Knowing she shouldn't, Ivy let him steer her toward the dance floor on an outdoor deck overlooking the Gulf of Mexico. "Seriously? My mother never mentioned my marital status?"

Without answering, he swung her into his arms. They moved easily into the rhythm provided by the small combo playing just inside the open double doors. Music flowed freely around them, accompanied by the muted murmur of voices and the rattle of silver and crystal. It was a romantic setting, all right. Ivy had no business whatsoever being here with a man other than her husband, especially a man who was so attentive. He was also a good dancer.

She could hardly remember the last time she'd managed to get Jack onto a dance floor. When her husband wanted to "hug" her, he was inclined to cut straight to the chase and not waste time *dancing*.

Of course, back when he was courting her, everything had been different. She sighed.

Bart swept her into a turn and resumed the conversation. "You know Joan," he said with amusement in his voice. "Your mother has a selective memory. I don't think she considers your marriage to be much of an impediment."

"I have a wonderful marriage," Ivy said staunchly.

"Really." He maneuvered her more closely against him. "So what kind of husband lets his wife go trailing off to Florida without him?"

"The kind who's busy," Ivy replied lightly, trying to keep her distance. Without success.

"What's he do?"

"He's a pilot for Alar Airlines. Right now he's... hmm, somewhere between Dallas and New York City would be my best guess." Why was she feeling this little thrill of excitement? She wasn't really tempted by Bart; of course not. A long-married woman such as herself...

"While his beautiful wife is off all alone to comfort her mother in her time of need," Bart murmured, his lips brushing Ivy's hair. "The man, quite simply, is a fool."

She wished she could argue. She wished she'd never met Bart.

She wished she wasn't so ticked at her husband that she'd listen to this kind of seditious talk.

Okay, they'd parted angrily, but was it Ivy's fault her mother had fallen and broken her leg? Was it Ivy's fault the timing was so bad, a few lousy weeks before their seventh wedding anniversary on Valentine's Day?

When she'd informed Jack that she had to rush to her mother's side, he'd been predictably unsympathetic. This, in turn, got *her* dander up.

"What else can I do?" she'd said, berating him. "Shoot her? I'll be home in plenty of time for our cruise."

Ah, their Caribbean cruise: a second honeymoon that would only have to reach mediocre to surpass their first, spent mostly in airports during the worst blizzard of the century. A cruise was just what they needed to put a little romance back into their increasingly humdrum marriage—yes, humdrum!

If Ivy had been unwilling to admit it before, she now found herself in a situation that forced her to reconsider. She hadn't wanted to believe she and Jack were growing apart, although that possibility had been pointed out to them by friends on innumerable occasions.

"Jack's no fool," she declared rather belatedly, responding to Bart's criticism. "He just . . . has a lot of responsibilities."

"With a mother-in-law like Joan, I'm sure he was *eager* to come along," Bart agreed.

She didn't know if he was putting her on or what. "Something like that," she muttered, "but it was impossible. He'll be using all his vacation time next month when we go on our cruise."

"A cruise, huh? Second honeymoon?"

I hope. "Of course—actually, anniversary. Our seventh." *Shut up, Ivy!*

"What ship?"

"The *Inamorata II*."

"Leaving from Puerto Rico? You'll like it, I guarantee."

She leaned back to look up into his face. She'd never much liked men with mustaches, but on Bart it looked just right. Or maybe she was at the point where anything would look good. "You know the ship?"

He nodded. "I was last on her almost three years ago, which is far too long. I'll have to remedy that one of these days."

The music ended, and he let her go with a reluctance she felt like an echo. What was wrong with her? She did *not* lust after other men; she loved her husband.

She loved her husband and he loved her!

"IVY, YOU MUST LISTEN to your mother."

Joan reclined like Cleopatra on a chaise longue on the deck of her luxurious condominium overlooking the same sparkling water that had been the scene of Ivy's temptation the previous evening. Joan sipped daintily at a small cup containing heavily sugared and creamed coffee, her silky blue robe draped gracefully around the leg cast.

"Yes, Mother." Ivy rolled her eyes and settled back in her own comfortable padded chair. In the clear light of day, she felt downright foolish for becoming so unstrung last night.

Yes, Bart Van Horn was an attractive man, a few years older than Jack's thirty-four and light-years more sophisticated. But she, Ivy Eileen Jensen Conrad, had resisted!

When Bart had drawn her into the shadows and into his arms, he hadn't known she was married. When he'd kissed her until her head whirled, he hadn't known she was married. When he slid one hand over her breast, leaned her back and nibbled on her ear, he hadn't known she was married.

She, on the other hand, *had*.

And she'd by-gosh come to her senses the minute he'd whispered something about the great view from his town house. Well, maybe not the *very* minute, but soon thereafter....

Joan's baby blue eyes narrowed thoughtfully. "I mean it, Ivy. Listen to me! You have nothing to berate yourself for. Jock's taking you for granted. Anybody could see that."

Jack had accused *Ivy* of taking *him* for granted, she recalled. "How can you purport to know anything about Jack?" she asked her mother mildly. "It's been more than a year since you've even seen him."

Joan sniffed haughtily. "Whose fault is that?"

"I'd say about half yours and half his." *With me in the middle, trying to keep peace.*

"Oh, no, you don't! You're not laying any blame on me." Joan shook her blond head vigorously. "Men will be men, Ivy, and that's a fact of nature. Here you are, beating up on yourself because you met an attractive man last night and let him—"

"I am not beating myself up." Belatedly Ivy added, "And I certainly didn't *let* him do anything. Good heavens, Mother, drop it. I'll never see Bart Van Horn again."

"Would you like to?"

"No!"

"Even after what happened?"

"Nothing happened."

"You call that kiss nothing? Does that mean you're used to kissing men other than your husband?"

Ivy, who'd never kissed another man except Jack since the day she met him, up to but not including last night, felt humiliation blaze in her cheeks. "Who told you?" she demanded.

"Never mind that. The fact of the matter is, you shared a passionate kiss with a man other than your husband. Which confirms something I already knew— you and Jake should never have married."

"That's an awful thing to say. You have no right—"

"I have a mother's right," Joan interrupted dramatically, pressing one fist above her heart in a histrionic gesture. "He's never put your interests above his own. With him it's all airplanes and cheap adrenaline rushes. Do you want to live this way for the rest of your life?"

No, Ivy did not. What she wanted was the Jack she'd married, the dashing and romantic Jack who'd swept her off her feet and into marriage within three months of their first meeting.

She wanted flowers and candy and diamonds and champagne, long intimate dinners and even longer intimate talks with her best friend, her lover...her husband.

But alas, she could understand where her mother was coming from. "Mother," she said gently, "are we talking about me or you?"

Joan caught her breath sharply. "Don't be cruel, Ivy."

"I'm not. Honestly I'm not." Sliding from her chair, Ivy dropped to her knees beside her mother's chaise and caught the older woman's hands in her own. "I love you, and I know you love me, but in this instance I don't want to follow in your footsteps."

"Ivy Eileen!"

"Mother, you've been married and divorced five times!"

"Only four divorces. Your father died on me."

"Okay, get technical. It was only a matter of time and you know it. My point is, your advice, however well-meaning, is...suspect."

"I've forgotten more about men than you'll ever know." Joan sniffed.

"Not about *my* man, and certainly not about my marriage. Jack and I pride ourselves on working out our problems together. We're equal partners in our marriage. We *communicate.*" Ivy resisted the urge to cross her fingers behind her back and add, "Or at least we used to."

"Does that mean you're going to tell him about Bart Van Horn the minute you get home?" Joan inquired slyly.

"I would, if there was anything to tell," Ivy said, flushed with success at standing up to her mother even semisuccessfully. "Why not? Nothing happened!"

"I beg to differ," Joan said. "You, my darling daughter, came face-to-face with temptation. It's called the seven-year itch and you've got it." She cupped Ivy's face with her hands and spoke with absolute certainty. "And if that husband of yours doesn't scratch it—"

"He will," Ivy said fervently. "Trust me, he will."

BART TELEPHONED LATER, but Ivy declined to take the call. All day her sense of righteousness continued to grow; a rich, handsome, worldly man had tried to hit on her and she'd stood firm.

She had every right to be proud. With her mother off lunching with Sherman, a pensive Ivy stood alone on the deck surrounded by the verdant green-and-gold beauty of Florida, Jack on her mind. Poor Jack, left alone back home in dreary Dallas.

It was raining when she'd left six days ago. It was probably raining still. The skies would be gray, the grass brown, the atmosphere dreary.

Suddenly she felt such an overpowering sense of love for her husband that she gasped and clutched the wooden railing with rigid fingers. She wasn't due to return home for another two days, but her mother was sufficiently recovered that there was no real need to delay.

She'd go home early and surprise him. She could just imagine his delight at her unanticipated arrival. Smiling, she hurried to the telephone. She'd have to call the airport to check the status of the next plane to Dallas, see if there was any room for her....

I'm coming home, Jack, she thought with growing excitement. *I'm coming home the same true-blue little wife I was when I left!*

And not a moment too soon.

JACK CONRAD STRODE through the throng at Dallas-Fort Worth International Airport, eyes facing forward with his suitcase-on-wheels bumping along behind him. Tiffani Welch had to break into a run to catch up with him.

"Jack, Jack, wait up!" she called out when she managed to get near enough to be heard.

He hesitated, turning to peruse the people who eddied and flowed around him. It gave her the time she needed to reach his side.

She smiled up at him flirtatiously. "What's your hurry? Going to a fire?"

He frowned. "Just heading home."

"Little woman waiting for you or what?" Tiffani hoped she didn't sound *too* scornful.

"As a matter of fact, no. Ivy's visiting her mother in Florida and won't be home for a couple of days."

He'd shoved his captain's hat back on his head and dark, curly hair spilled over his broad forehead. His eyes were brown, a velvety brown that turned Tiffani to mush every time he looked at her. Damn, the guy was drop-dead gorgeous.

Fortunately he didn't even seem to know it.

"Too bad," she said insincerely. "You're probably...lonely."

He shrugged. "Yeah, well, I guess. Did you want something, Tiff?"

Ohhh, baby! She fumbled around in the pocket of her fuchsia and gray flight attendant's uniform. "You know that little kid I brought up to visit you in the cockpit?"

"Yeah?" Was that suspicion on his face?

"He wanted me to give you this." Tiffani pulled a folded scrap of paper from her pocket and offered it to him triumphantly. She'd had to practically stand over the little brat with a baseball bat to get him to "express his gratitude to the nice captain."

Three sodas stuffed with maraschino cherries had finally done the trick; she hoped the little monster would pay for that.

Jack took the folded bit of paper and opened it. The kid had drawn a sorry excuse for an airplane, but Jack's broad grin declared it wonderful. "Thanks," he said with more enthusiasm than she'd seen hitherto. "I'll save this to show Ivy."

Tiffani grimaced. "That pink stuff on the edge is maraschino juice," she offered. "I think."

"Yeah. Thanks again." He cocked his head and waited.

"Uhh..." She glanced toward the Alar flight crew coming toward them on the concourse. "A few of us are going out for pizza a little later. Would you like to... join us?"

For a moment he hesitated, and she'd have sworn he was about to say yes, then thought better of it. With the first negative turn of his head, she jumped in.

"Just a pizza and a chance to relax with friends," she pressed. "You said yourself you had nothing to go home to."

"That's not exactly..." He sighed, lifting his broad shoulders in the beautifully fitted gray uniform. Jack Conrad was a man made to wear a uniform, or nothing at all.

"Come *on,* Jack!" She slid her hand beneath his arm and turned him toward the approaching group, adding coquettishly, "Unless you think somebody's gonna bite you."

His arm beneath her light touch felt like steel. He gave her a quick glance that looked a little cautious, a little sheepish. Then he grinned.

"Sure, why not?" he said. "Pizza and a beer with friends is probably just what I need."

For starters, Tiffani thought, trying to hide her elation.

"THIS TIME, I've got him!"

Tiffani grabbed her best friend, Amber, by the arms and squeezed so hard Amber yelped in pain. The two young flight attendants stood alone, whispering in the women's lounge at the T. Total Texas Tavern.

Amber pulled away and rubbed her arms. "I don't know, Tiff. I've never heard of Jack Conrad fooling around."

"That could just mean he's smart enough to be sneaky."

"Yeah, smart enough *not* to."

"Smart enough not to get caught." Tiffani grinned. "Did you know his wife's out of town?"

"No kidding!" Amber looked thoughtful. "Even so—"

"If you can't say something encouraging, don't say anything at all." Tiffani dug around in her miniback-pack, looking for her lipstick. "I've been after that guy for months and I have a very strong feeling that tonight's the night!"

FLYING STAND-BY, Ivy arrived at DFW in the middle of the night. She was tired, rumpled and travel stained, but triumphant, too.

She was going home to her marriage and her husband. Sure, she and Jack had gotten into the habit of treating each other like old shoes, but that was about to change. She'd seen the light and was sure he would, too—just as soon as she pointed it out to him.

They loved each other. That's all that mattered, right? Not whether another man had made her pulse race; not whether another woman—

Ivy smiled fondly. If there was one thing you had to say for Jack Conrad, he was true-blue. Jack wouldn't even look at another woman. She'd have staked her life on that.

Her car waited in the long-term parking lot. Having had a lot of practice, she retrieved it in record time. Pulling away from the airport, she anticipated Jack's joy.

Assuming he was home. That was a sobering thought. There'd been a lot of flu going around when she left. Although Jack never got sick, there was a strong possibility he might be picking up flights from pilots downed by the bug. Maybe she should have called him. Damn! It was going to be a big disappointment if he wasn't there to be surprised.

The drive home would have taken forty minutes during traffic, but in the dead of night it only took twenty-five. They lived on a cul-de-sac overlooking a golf course in a big brick house in an upscale development full of other big brick houses. Apparently someone in the neighborhood was having a party or houseguests, she thought, pulling into her driveway. Several strange cars were parked at the curb.

She didn't want to take a chance on spoiling the surprise, so she didn't park in the garage with its noisy door. Taking only her purse, she crept from her car and walked quietly around to the front of the house. Cutting across the grass, moisture squished beneath her shoes, but she didn't change her course.

At the entry she slipped the key into the lock and swung the door open on smooth oiled hinges. So far so good. Inside, she stepped out of her shoes and walked on silent feet toward the master bedroom at the end of the hallway. Muted light spilled from beneath a half-open door, her first assurance that her husband was home.

She hesitated just outside the bedroom, smiling in anticipation. Reaching for the doorknob, she became aware of the sound of rushing water in the shower, and then Jack's loud, uncertain baritone: *O sole meeee-o . . .*

It was the only song he knew, and he only sang it when he thought he had the world on a string. Well, she was here to make his good mood even better.

Flinging open the door, her husband's voice ringing in her ears, she stepped triumphantly into the room.

And got the shock of her life.

2

IVY SCREAMED.

She clenched her hands into fists and stamped her feet and screamed at the top of her lungs.

That was all the encouragement the naked blonde in Ivy's bed needed. *She* screamed, too. Sitting up with the sheet clutched over obviously bare breasts, she shrieked like a banshee.

Ivy *felt* like a banshee. With a murderous rage rising like a red tide, she was on the verge of losing it completely. Taking a threatening step toward the cowering woman in her bed, Ivy opened her mouth to demand answers.

The words were never uttered, for at that moment the bathroom door was flung open and Jack barreled through. Clutching a thick blue terry towel around his waist, he managed to spray drops of water everywhere.

"Who—what—where—?" Jack spotted his wife and skidded to a stop, a big smile blossoming on his face. "Ivy! Darling!"

Then, as if locking on to a beacon, his gaze followed her glare and he spotted the woman in the bed. His smile fled as if it had never been, to be replaced by a kind of shocked horror. "Tiffani? Holy shhhh— *Tiffani!*"

Tiffani leapt from the bed, her bare behind a creamy flash as she dashed toward the bathroom. "Out of my way!" she shrieked, pushing him aside and lunging through the doorway. "She's crazy! She's going to kill me!" The door slammed.

"Not right away," Ivy shouted, starting forward. "First I'm going to kill Jack! *Then* I'm going to kill you, you little—"

Jack made a grab for his furious wife. "Ivy, this isn't how it looks!"

"Don't touch me!" She flung his hands aside, unable to bear his polluted touch after he'd sullied himself with another woman. "It's exactly how it looks." She sucked in a trembling breath, feeling righteous indignation swell beneath the outrage. "You animal! This is the thanks I get for—"

She stopped short, realizing she was about to say *for resisting the seven-year itch,* substituting "—for coming home early to surprise you. I guess we know who got surprised!"

"But honey—but sweetheart—" He made fumbling motions toward her with his hands, and the towel dropped around his ankles.

"Don't you honey-sweetheart *me.*" She glared at him. There he stood, naked as a jaybird, every muscular inch on fulsome display. She'd just bet he'd knocked that blonde for a loop. Despair and disappointment overwhelmed her and she groaned. "How could you, Jack? Oh, how could you?"

"I didn't. I swear to God, I didn't." He shoved wet, curly hair off his face distractedly. "I don't know what she was doing in my bed, honest."

Ivy turned her back on him. She was trembling so badly she had to grip the tall footboard of the bed for support. "Do strange women turn up regularly in our—*your* bed when I'm out of town? Wait a minute!" She snapped her fingers, whirling to face him. "She's not all that strange, right? You called her—what was it? The name of some store—" A couple more finger snaps while he stood there looking miserable, head hanging and shoulders slumping. "Macy? Gimbel? Wal-Mart?"

"Her name's Tiffani," he muttered. "She's a flight attendant at Alar."

"That's what you think! What she *is* is dead, because I'm going to kill her." Striding past him, Ivy tried the bathroom door; finding it locked, she banged her fists on the panel. "Come out of there, you—you home wrecker! Face me like a man!"

From inside the bathroom, a wail arose. "Keep her away from me, Jack! If she lays a finger on me, I'll sue!"

"Tiffani—"

"I mean it!"

"Ivy, let's go into the other room." He put his hands on her shoulders and tried to drag her away.

She whirled on him, eyes blurred with tears to the point where she could hardly see him. Which was actually a help, because it spared her from having to look too closely at his deceitful, lying face.

"I told you not to touch me," she cried.

"I'm innocent, Ivy. I swear it."

His voice sounded sincere enough, but how could you believe anything a naked man might say? "Yeah," she choked out, "you and O.J." She rubbed the heels of her hands over her eyes and drew a ragged breath.

So now she could see him again in all his bare-assed glory. "Will you put something on?" she exclaimed in exasperation.

He lunged for the towel in a sodden pile on the carpet and wrapped it around his waist again. She had the feeling that he'd do just about anything she told him to do at this point. She toyed with the idea of a Lord Godiva trek through north Dallas just for the hell of it.

From the bathroom came another plaintive call. "Is it safe to come out? Is she gone?"

Ivy opened her mouth to rain curses upon the blond head of this usurper, then realized she'd be wasting her breath. If Jack really valued his marriage, no temptation on earth could have brought him to this pass.

So Ivy said, "She's gone—into the living room. If you've got the sense of a gnat, you'll be gone, too— out of this house and out of my life for the rest of yours." She added with dark menace, "Which will be extremely short if I ever so much as hear of you even looking at—" she glared at Jack "—my ex-husband!"

And with a toss of her head, Ivy stalked out of the room and straight to the wet bar in the family room, where she poured herself a stiff vodka and tonic and confronted the end of the world.

THE SOFT SNICK of an opening door brought Ivy swinging around to confront the enemy. She would not, however, do so verbally—unless forced into it. She couldn't afford to lose control again, as she'd done a few minutes earlier. She wasn't going to let them put her on the defensive when she was the injured party.

The blond bimbo crept into sight, hugging the far wall of the hallway. She'd thrown on jeans and a skimpy little orange T-shirt and carried her shoes and a jacket in her hands.

She hesitated. "Mrs. Conrad—"

"Get out," Ivy said, memorizing everything in case she decided to put out a contract on this little twit at some future date: the big blond hair, the big blue eyes, the big orange—

Jack appeared in the hallway beside his paramour. "You'd better go, Tiffani," he said in a distraught voice. He wore jeans and nothing more. The SOB looked like a Greek god, right up to and including chiseled features hard as marble.

If Ivy recalled her mythology, Greek gods had fooled around a lot, too.

"Jack," the blonde whined, "let me expl—"

"Jeez, haven't you done enough already?" Jack's tense expression tightened still more. "You're killin' me, here, Tiff."

Ivy snorted.

Tiffani slunk out. Jack watched her go before turning toward his glowering wife.

"You've got to let me explain, Ivy."

"Seems pretty self-explanatory, actually."

"But it's not what you think."

She widened her eyes. "What could I possibly think? I come home early to surprise my husband and find a naked blonde in my bed and my husband singing in the shower as if he'd just—" She was talking too fast, losing control again. She sucked in a deep, anguished breath.

"It wasn't like that at all," Jack said. He looked as if he wanted to grab her and make her listen. Her expression must have disabused him of that notion, for he turned instead to the bar. Pouring a couple of inches of vodka into a water glass, he tossed it down.

"Jack," she said sarcastically, "you don't drink. It's bad for your reflexes, you said."

"I'll have another," he said, and did.

She shrugged. "Suit yourself. What you do is no longer of even peripheral interest to me."

He shuddered with the impact of the straight vodka on his unprepared stomach. "Don't say that," he pleaded in thick tones. "She followed me home. She said I'd forgotten to pick up my change at the bar—"

"Aha!" Vindication! "You admit you were at a bar with her!"

He blinked as if his vision had become a little fuzzy. Was the vodka already hitting him? "Well, sure, why not? Me'n'...some other people." He shook his head as if to clear it. "I thanked her and told her to let herself out 'cause I had to take a shower and...stuff."

"You're so polite," Ivy agreed with bitter approbation, "not to mention *clean.*"

"Yeah, well, I hopped in the shower and the next thing I knew you were screamin' your head off and she's headin' buck-naked into the bathroom. I'm as shocked as you are, Ivy. I'm just an innocent victim, here, I swear to God."

Ivy gritted her teeth. "That is the lamest story I ever heard," she stated. "Do you really expect me to believe it?"

Jack opened his mouth and she saw him form the words: *Of course!* But then his head drooped and he groaned. "It does sound kinda feeble," he admitted. "But it's the gods' truth, Ivy, sweetheart, baby. Why would I want a little piece'a fluff like that when I've got you?"

He took a step toward her, a weaving step. So he *was* feeling the effects of the vodka, and who knew what else he'd consumed at the bar with little Miss—

"That's just the point," she snapped at him, easily evading his outstretched hands. "You *didn't* have me. What is it with you, Jack? When you're not with the one you love, do you just conveniently love the one you're with?"

He blinked big blurry brown eyes. "I love *you,*" he said plaintively.

"I don't think so." She set her now-empty glass on the bar and picked up her purse.

"You love *me.*"

"I'm going to have to take that under advisement." She started for the front door.

He followed. "Where you goin', Ivy? Hey, don't leave me!"

At the front door she turned, her head held high. "I'm going to a motel," she announced dramatically.

"But—but—" He glanced around helplessly, his big hands clenching and unclenching in front of his bare, ridged abdomen. "This is home. You can't—"

"You don't think so?" She gripped her envelope-style purse with tense fingers, afraid she'd smack him upside the head with it if she didn't. "Jack Conrad, you've forfeited any right you ever had to tell me what I can or cannot do."

"But, Ivy! We need to talk!"

"Tomorrow."

"Do you mean it?"

She couldn't bear to look at him any longer. She opened the door. "Tomorrow," she said. "And if you're even half-smart, you'll have a better story worked out than the one you tried to hand me tonight!"

UNFORTUNATELY, he didn't have a better story. He seemed determined to stick to the same weak tale of uninvited female aggression. Ivy was in no mood to be generous, exhausted from a sleepless night of anguished speculation.

It looked as if Jack hadn't fared much better; he looked like hell. He peered at her through bloodshot eyes and offered her coffee with hands that trembled. Knowing how his coffee tasted even under the best of circumstances, she declined. Tossing her purse onto the kitchen counter, she faced him with narrow eyes and an even narrower mind.

He shuffled his feet. "So where'd you spend the night, honey?"

"At the Holiday Inn, and don't you 'honey' me, you—you cad."

He shoved errant curls away from his face, his movements distracted. "Ivy, I'm innocent. She followed me home uninvited."

"After an evening spent drinking and carousing. I don't suppose that could have given her any encouragement."

"I told you, we were with a bunch of other Alar people. I only went because I was lonely. I missed you, baby." He took a tentative step in her direction but the look on her face stopped him in his tracks.

"My point exactly. You missed me so much you decided to try a substitute."

"It wasn't that way. Jeez, Ivy, it was just a simple beer or two at the T. Total Texas Tavern—"

"That body exchange!"

He blinked. "Huh?"

"Everybody's heard about that place, so don't play dumb with me."

"Who's playing?"

"You, big boy, but not with me." She planted her hands on her hips. "I did a lot of thinking last night... Don't look so hopeful! None of it benefited *you.*"

"Oh." His face drooped.

"I've come to the conclusion that I'm not ready to come to a conclusion. I've...got to get past the hurt." She glared at him. "If that's possible."

"Ah, Ivy..." He looked at her with sheep's eyes. "This is all a horrible misunderstanding. Why can't you trust me, sweetheart?"

She stared at him in disbelief. "After finding a naked woman in our bed? That's asking a lot, don't you think?"

"Well, yes, but...I told you the truth, may God strike me dead if I'm lying."

Ivy glanced quickly toward the ceiling, expecting a bolt of lightning to render him deceased. She was strangely disappointed when it didn't. Poetic justice, apparently, would not be hers today.

Suddenly inspired, she said, "What if the tables were turned?"

He frowned. "Like how?"

"Like, what if you'd walked in and found a naked man in our bed and me singing like an idiot in the shower? Would you be so willing to believe he followed me home and jumped in my bed when my back was turned?"

"Well, I . . . might." It was a struggle for him to get the words out. "Damn, Ivy, I know you'd never get yourself into a mess like this. You're too smart. And you're loyal and trustworthy and faithful—"

"That's not a woman you're describing, that's a dog," she cut in, thrusting aside memories of a certain Florida land developer. A simple kiss—*completely unsolicited*—was hardly in the same category as blatant cheating. "You make me sound like Lassie," she added.

"*I'm* loyal and trustworthy and faithful, too," he said. "I'm just not too smart. I knew Tiffani—"

"The blond bimbo."

"—was kinda after my frame." He looked embarrassed by the admission. "But I couldn't see any problem if I wasn't alone with her. In retrospect, I shouldn't have gone to that bar—"

"The least of your transgressions."

"—but I *didn't* invite her home with me."

"I don't believe you."

"It's true!"

They stared at each other, or rather, he stared and she glared. At last he sighed.

"I was afraid that would be your attitude so I took the liberty—"

She understood instantly. "You didn't! You've got your floozie here?" She glanced around, her hackles rising.

He looked even more uncomfortable. "I wish you wouldn't call her names."

"I'm going to call *you* names if you don't—"

"Okay, take it easy." He raised his voice. "You can come out now, Tiffani."

Ivy stood as if turned to stone, waiting for the appearance of her rival. Slowly the door to the walk-in pantry swung open and a blond head poked through.

"Is it safe?"

The woman's frightened gaze settled on Ivy, who growled deep in her throat, but stood her ground.

Jack nodded. "Come on out and *tell* her, Tiffani."

Tiffani edged into the room, fortunately a good ten feet from where Ivy stood like a frozen lump. Except for the blond hair, Ivy would never have recognized her with her clothes on: jeans and a sloppy oversize sweater that reached almost to her knees.

Yeah, that disguise really fools me, Ivy thought.

Tiffani cleared her throat. "Uhh...it's just like Jack—Captain Conrad said."

Ivy arched a skeptical brow. "Oh? And what exactly does that cover, *dear?*"

"He—I—well, we—" The woman glanced nervously at Jack.

Ivy smiled coldly. "Exactly."

"No, uh...I did follow him home. I mean, after he went to the bar with us I thought he was interested. I mean, how could he miss the signals I was sending him?" Tiffani glanced at Jack, who looked stricken by this line of "explanation."

"I mean, how, indeed?" Ivy concurred past a breaking heart. Somehow, some part of her had still clung to the hope that Jack could wiggle out of this noose.

Tiffani edged a step away. "When I got here, he was nice enough and all. But he just took his change and told me to let myself out, that he was about to get in the shower. I mean, is that lame?" She cast him a puzzled glance. "He wasn't even wearing a shirt. It was practically an invitation, right?"

Jack choked. "Tiffani, you're doing it again! I never invited you to stay. On the level now, okay?"

Her expression brightened. "Yes, that's true. You never did—in so many words." She swung her attention back to Ivy. "Believe me, if I'd had any idea you were even in the same state, I would never have—"

"Get out," Ivy said. "Get out before I snatch all that blond hair out by its black roots."

Tiffani backed toward the door. "Would it help if I said I'm sorry?"

"Not a damned bit. You're sorry you got caught, that's all."

Jack stepped between them. "But nothing happened!" he yelled. "Tell her, Tiffani!"

Tiffani's eyes widened. "Didn't I mention that? Nothing happened, Mrs. Conrad. You got here in the nick of time." She glanced at Jack. "Did I do okay?"

With a strangled cry, Ivy made a dive for her tormentor. Jack caught his wife and held her back while the blond bombshell made a hasty exit. With her quarry no longer in sight, Ivy jerked away from her unfaithful husband's grip.

"That didn't quite work out the way I'd hoped." He looked miserable, but he continued doggedly. "Ivy, listen, this is the truth. I did not sleep with that woman. I've never slept with any woman but you since the day we met. I love you."

She curled her lip. "Next you'll tell me you weren't even tempted."

His hesitation was so slight that only her hyper vigilance detected it. "Never," he vowed.

"Liar!" If *she'd* been tempted, she damned well knew he had been, too. Only she hadn't acted on it. *She* had honored her marriage vows.

"Ivy—"

"Get out!"

"Ivy, trust me."

"In your dreams, mister. Get out."

"I'm innocent!"

"Get out!"

"But this is my house."

"No, this is *my* house and I don't want you in it anymore. Go away, Jack. Go away and let me figure out what I'm going to do next."

"Ivy—"

"Get out or the next words I utter will be to a good divorce lawyer."

He got out.

3

AT TIMES LIKE THESE, a girl needed her mother.

Even a mother like Joan Jensen, who was bound to say "I told you so" before she even understood the problem.

Alone in her now-tarnished home, weeping and miserable, Ivy finally picked up the telephone and dialed her mother in Florida.

She knew it was the wrong thing to do but she simply couldn't help herself. At Joan's jaunty "Hello," a fresh gale of sobs shook Ivy.

"Mo-o-o-other!"

"Good Lord, is that you, Ivy? What has that swine done to you now?"

"He...he...he's been un*faith*ful!"

"Aha!"

Ivy could almost see her mother's triumphant expression. Past transgressions had been more of the "He forgot my birthday!" or the "He loves football more than he loves me!" variety. This one was the biggie.

Joan rushed into a monologue no doubt intended to be comforting. "Don't cry, sweetheart. He's not worth it. No man is. They're just alike, every one of them. Jack's no worse than the rest of his ilk—and no better, either. They'll string you along and the first chance they get they go astray with some little—''

"Mother! You're not helping matters with that kind of talk," Ivy sobbed.

"Of course I'm helping. Once you have a chance to think about it, you'll see that I'm offering you the wisdom of the ages. Men will be men, darling girl. Jump on the next airplane and rush back here to mother. I'll have you feeling better in nothing flat.''

You'll have me suicidal in nothing flat, Ivy thought. "I c-can't," she blubbered. "I've got responsibilities—''

"Responsibilities my great-aunt Hattie.''

"Really." Ivy swallowed back her tears, which immediately transformed into hiccups. "See, I'm feeling better already. I just needed to dump on someone.''

"That's what mothers are for, darling. Now tell me all the gory details. Did you catch him in the act?''

"P-practically. He said he was a victim of circumstances, that this—this *girl* just sort of followed him home like a puppy dog and when he turned his back, jumped naked into his bed.''

Silence greeted that explanation. Then Joan said, "Well, that's not the dumbest story I ever heard. Your father once tried to convince me—''

"This is *my* disaster," Ivy wailed, "not yours!''

"I stand corrected. So if you don't want to come home and you don't want my advice, just exactly why did you call, Ivy?''

"B-because I need some *there-there!*''

"That, I can provide. There, there, sweetie, this, too, shall pass. What a louse—and after you passed up a chance to see Bart Van Horn's etchings. And after you've given Jake the best years of your life...."

Listening to her mother's indignant drone, Ivy slowly began to feel better, much to her surprise. She'd survive this ultimate betrayal; of course she would. She came from sturdy stock. Why, her mother had survived five marriages and who knew how many close calls?

Of course, Ivy had never aspired to her mother's marital standard. She'd married Jack with every intention of spending the rest of her life with him. Now that he'd been unfaithful to her, she had to wonder if perhaps her mother might have the right idea after all—love 'em and leave 'em before they can leave you.

THERE WAS ABSOLUTELY no chance that Ivy would ever sleep in *that bed* again: none, nada, forget it. In fact, there seemed slight chance she'd ever be able to sleep in that *room* again.

Especially after the purge.

First she hauled out all of Jack's things—clothing, shoes, sports gear, odds and ends—and tossed them into the driveway. That felt good; really good.

Then she dragged all the linens off the offending bed, added them to the pile and set fire to it. When the fire engine responded to neighbors' calls with sirens blaring, she expressed great shock and unending gratitude for their prompt intervention. Why, she had no idea how those things had caught fire! Thank you, thank you, thank you, she gushed.

Next she called a used furniture dealer and in the blink of an eye, the wayward bedroom was as empty as that blond babe's sense of decency. Sitting on the floor in the middle of the denuded room, a jug of wine and a goblet before her, Ivy considered her options.

She could divorce him.

She *should* divorce him.

If she had a shred of self-respect or pride, she *would* divorce him.

On the other hand, she argued with herself, this was his first transgression—that she knew of. True, it was a lulu. It was much more serious than a kiss, or even a pass. This was the big enchilada, the whole shooting match.

Would she ever be able to put her arms around him again—she shuddered—without remembering?

And yet...and yet, she yearned to forgive him, yearned to return to their previous relationship—not the relationship they'd had when she'd left for Florida, but earlier than that.

Jack's job as a pilot and her sometime-job as a personal shopper for one of the biggest and most exclusive department stores in Dallas had somehow become more important than their relationship.

She'd known they were growing apart but she'd resisted the notion. She'd believed there was still time to put their marriage first instead of last.

Now it appeared she'd been wrong...but maybe not. Despite this betrayal, she found herself reluctant to write *finis* to the most rewarding chapter in her life.

Could she actually still *care* for him?

If she did, so what? They'd never be able to work this out, not as long as she felt so...so...so morally *superior*. There simply was no way to get past this horrible betrayal.

Or was there?

"SHE ACTUALLY PILED all your stuff in the driveway and threw a match at it?"

Rob Harris paused with a beer in one hand and a can opener in the other, staring at his old buddy Jack Conrad.

Jack nodded miserably. He still couldn't believe he was confiding something so personal, even to his best friend. But he also knew that if he didn't get it off his chest, he might explode.

Rob handed over the beer. "So what'd you do to deserve it, man? Get caught with a naked blonde?" He guffawed.

"Yeah," Jack said, relieved he wouldn't have to be the one who said it. "That's about it."

That wiped the smirk off Rob's face fast enough. "Shee-it!" He glanced toward the door leading to the hall, which in turn led to the kitchen where his wife, Cathy, hummed as she whipped up another of her gourmet dinners. "I think you better explain that one," he said in a much lower tone.

So Jack did. When he explained how lonesome he was with his wife in Florida, Rob nodded sympathetically. When Jack described how he dreaded going back to that big empty house, Rob nodded sympathetically.

When Jack described how uninterested he really had been when a pretty little blond Alar flight attendant "who shall remain nameless" had talked him into going to the T. Total Texas with "the gang," Rob came to attention.

"Tiffani Welch," Rob prophesied.

"Well, hell," Jack said, disgusted. "I didn't mean to name any names."

"Damned gentlemanly of you," Rob soothed, "but hell, everybody knows she's been chasing you. She even bragged to the other flight attendants that she'd get you into bed if it was the last thing she ever did."

"Well, hell," Jack said again, pacing around the room. "Don't you think you might have warned me?"

"Why?" Rob looked genuinely surprised. "You knew it. You're married not dead."

That stopped Jack in his tracks. *Had* he known all along? Was he as innocent as he'd claimed, as innocent as he'd tried to convince Ivy?

What would have happened if Ivy had stayed in Florida?

Rob took a slug of beer. "So our little blond vixen had her way with you. How'd Ivy find out?"

"No, she didn't have her way with me. But that may have been due to blind, stupid—" He couldn't say *luck,* not considering the mess he was in at the moment.

He resumed pacing, the whole sordid story spilling out, right up to and including Ivy's unannounced appearance.

At which point Rob let out a long, low whistle. "You're lucky to be alive," he said.

"The jury's still out on that. Ivy spent the night in a motel, then showed up at the house the next morning and tossed me and Tiffani both out on our—"

Rob made a strangled sound. "You let Tiffani spend the night there after—?"

"No! What kind of moron do you think I am?" Jack stopped short; it was painfully obvious what kind of moron Rob, his oldest and best friend, thought he was. "I called Tiff the next morning and asked her—

hell, I ordered her to come over and back me up, if necessary, when I talked to Ivy."

"It was necessary," Rob said.

"Yeah. Oh, yeah!" Jack frowned. "You don't suppose Ivy jumped to the same conclusion you did— that Tiffani spent the night there."

Rob threw up his hands. "Don't ask me to explain the female mind."

"Fat lot of help you are," Jack muttered. He finished his beer and put the bottle on a table. "So now Ivy's burned my stuff, sold all the bedroom furniture and she's treating me like a cow pie."

"Women. Can't live with 'em—"

For a few minutes the two men glumly considered the foibles of the female sex. Then Rob looked up with an expression of cautious optimism on his face.

"You know, there might be a way—"

Jack was eager to grasp at straws. "Name it!"

"Cathy and I could have you both to dinner."

Jack's shoulders slumped. "No chance. Number one, Ivy wouldn't come if she knew I was here. Number two, if she did come, she'd spend the entire evening yelling at me."

"No, she wouldn't—not in front of other people," Rob predicted confidently. "Her manners are too good. And while she's being civil, you can worm your way back into her heart."

"What's this about worming your way into whose heart?"

At the sound of Cathy's bemused voice, both Jack and Rob jumped guiltily.

"Hi, honey," Rob said too heartily. "Old Jack's in the doghouse with Ivy—"

"Ivy's home? I thought she was still in Florida. Good grief, we can't have dinner together without—" She reached for the telephone on the table.

"Hang on a minute, Cathy." Rob cast a surreptitious glance at his friend. "I said, Jack's in the doghouse. Just a little spat—nothing serious. But I was telling him that maybe you and I could help get them together again. You know, maybe have the two of them over for dinner soon to give them an excuse to kiss and make up."

"She's thrown him out of the house?" Cathy looked worried. "Is this something we should be involved in?"

"Hey," Rob said expansively, "what are friends for? She'll thank us for it." He glanced at Jack. "How about Friday night?"

"Anytime," Jack said fervently. "If you can get her here, I'll owe you big-time."

"Of course we can get her here. Right, Cathy? We'll just tell her Jack's flying to San Franciso or something and we knew she'd be alone. Hey, better yet, tell her I went with Jack and it'll be an evening of girl talk."

"Rob," Cathy protested, "I don't feel good about this. I don't want to deceive a friend."

"She'll thank you for it, sweetheart. Now here's what we'll do—"

As his best friend spun out little white lies with aplomb, Jack found himself daring to hope again.

RIGHT AWAY, Ivy knew something was going on. Cathy was a nervous wreck when she answered the door, and she spilled as much wine as she managed to pour into the goblets.

"Clumsy me," she said, offering a slightly sticky glass to Ivy. "Cheers."

"Cheers." Ivy sipped carefully. She had a very strong suspicion that she'd need to keep her wits about her tonight. "So what's for dinner?" She sniffed the air appreciatively and found it redolent of garlic and olive oil.

"Pasta. I've got a new recipe to try out on you."

"Are we eating before or after Rob and Jack show up?"

"Oh, after—" Cathy looked stricken. "You know? How? Oh, Ivy, I'm so sorry. I didn't mean to deceive you, but the guys said I'd be doing you a favor."

"How so?" Ivy didn't know whether to be angry or relieved. She'd refused to speak to Jack since she'd thrown him out of the house, which meant she had no idea what he might be up to.

"Because Jack wants to make up," Cathy said earnestly. "I'm sure you do, too."

"Do you know what we're fighting about?" Ivy kept her voice conversational, but it was a stretch.

"Well, no. But you two are so perfect together that I'm sure it must just be a misunderstanding."

"Did Jack tell you that?"

Cathy nodded. "In so many words. I didn't ask for specifics—I don't like to pry. But I know how much you two love each other so I'm sure whatever has happened—"

"Give it up, Cathy."

Cathy blinked in surprise. "Excuse me?"

"I came home unexpectedly and found a naked woman in our bed. I don't call that a little thing."

Cathy's mouth dropped open in appropriate horror. "Oh—oh! He *cheated* on you? Oh, Ivy!" She flung her arms around her friend, sloshing wine onto the beige carpet in the process. "He didn't! Did he really?"

"I saw it with my own eyes. A blonde in the bed and a bozo in the shower, singing at the top of his lungs. What would be your interpretation of that sequence of events?"

Cathy finally got hold of herself, but her hazel eyes gleamed with malice. "I'm going to kill Rob," she announced grimly.

"Why? He's just trying to help a friend, no matter how misguided."

"That's not why. I'm going to kill him because *he knows* and he didn't tell me, just set me up to do the dirty work."

Ivy sighed. "That was pretty tacky," she agreed.

"Just like a man."

"Now you sound like my mother."

"I always liked your mother, even if she is a little—"

The front door opened and a voice filled with false bravado rang through the house. "Hi, honey, I'm home. Our flight got canceled and guess who's with me?"

"Hello, Jack."

"Hello, Ivy. Uhh . . . hello, Cathy."

Cathy glared. "Don't speak to me, you louse."

"Hi, honey," Rob inserted hastily. "How's about a little kiss?"

"I wouldn't kiss you if you were the last man in Texas!"

"Uh-oh," Rob said. "What have I done now?"

"You set me up, that's what you did." Cathy marched to the wet bar and poured herself more wine. "You said these two had a 'little' problem. I don't consider your husband sleeping with another woman to be a 'little' problem. Apparently you do."

Rob looked as if he was about to break into a cold sweat. "No, of course not. I'd never think—"

"Maybe you've done it yourself and that's why you let that—" she glared at Jack "—that *philanderer* in our house."

"I'm innocent of all charges," Jack protested. "Bring out a stack of Bibles and I'll swear on 'em."

"Wait a minute," Rob said to Cathy. "You spilled the beans to Ivy?"

"No, dear." Sarcasm dripped from Cathy's tone. "*She* spilled the beans to me!"

"But how did you know Jack would be here?" Rob appealed to Ivy.

"It didn't exactly take a mental giant to see through this little scam," she said, rather enjoying seeing everyone at loggerheads. Misery really did love company, apparently.

Jack's smile looked hopeful. "But you came, anyway. Does that mean—?"

Ivy nodded. "It means I've made up my mind. I figured this was as good a time and place to tell you as any."

"Thank God." Jack sucked in a deep breath. "You're letting me come home!"

"No, Jack, I'm going on that cruise."

He did a double take, but recovered quickly. "Even better," he declared with enthusiasm. "That's what we need, to get away from it all and concentrate on each other. Isn't that what you kept telling me? Yeah, this is great, honey."

"I *told* you that for years, while you kept putting me off. Listen to what I'm telling you now, Jack! I said, I'm going on that cruise and I'm going alone."

A silence so total that they could hear the tick of the grandfather clock in the hallway settled over them. It was as if they were all holding their breaths in unison.

Finally Jack said, in a strangled tone, "But I don't understand."

"That's why I'm here," Ivy said gently, "to explain it to you. You see, Jack, we've got a real problem."

"I know, but I swore to you that I didn't lay a finger on her."

"I mean, an *additional* problem. The blonde's just a symptom." Ivy had spent hours thinking about this and spoke with great authority. "I feel morally superior to you, Jack. I don't respect you anymore. I can't possibly live with a man I don't respect."

"You *are* morally superior to me," he agreed eagerly. "Women are just naturally...*better* than men. Beat me up all you want for pure stupidity—I can take it. You'd never get yourself into this kind of mess. Don't you think I know that? Whatever punishment you've dreamed up for me—"

"Punishment, Jack? Don't be so melodramatic." But from the stunned and fascinated expressions on the faces of the Harrises as they listened, Jack wasn't the only one relying on melodrama.

"Innocent though I may be, I'm in no position to quibble," Jack said. "So tell me what it'll take to get you back home where I can make all this up to you?"

"All right, you asked for it." Ivy's plan was... diabolical, to say the least, but it sure as hell would even the score. "As I said, I'm going on that cruise alone."

"But...but you don't want to do that. What kind of fun can you have alone?" Jack's handsome face was screwed up with confusion.

"That's just it," Ivy said with malice aforethought. "I don't plan to be alone."

Jack glanced at Cathy. "Is she going with you?"

"That wouldn't be at all convenient, considering that I'm going on this cruise for the express purpose of having an affair."

"Having an—" Jack's voice slid smoothly from surprise to shock to a bass roar. "You mean you're going to sleep with some other guy?"

"That's exactly what I mean," Ivy said, calm as you please. "There's only one way I might be able to get past what you've done to me. What's sauce for the goose is sauce for the gander, Jack Conrad. I'm going on this cruise to sleep with another man. Once I've evened that score, then we can talk about our marriage...if we both still want to. And that's my final word on the subject."

4

"LIKE HELL it's your final word on the subject!"

Jack had never been so astounded in his life. If his wife thought he was going to sit back and let her sleep with the first good-looking guy she met, she had another think coming.

Rob looked equally horrified. "She doesn't mean it, Jack," he said. "She's just trying to make you feel even lousier than you already do."

"Lousier?" Cathy repeated. "Why should he feel lousy if he didn't do it? Are you innocent or not, Jack?"

"Stay out of this, babe," Rob recommended. "Let them work this—"

"I can't stay out of it!" She looked mad enough to tear into him with her fingernails. "You're the one who got me involved in the first place."

"I was just trying to help a friend who got a bum deal, that's all."

"Well, I'm just trying to help a friend who got a bum deal from *your* friend."

"Then you approve of her going off and sleeping with the first guy she meets, just to get even?" Rob demanded indignantly.

Jack took a menacing step forward, clenching his hands into fists. "Watch your mouth, fella. This really is none of your—"

"This is my house!" Rob threw out his arms in a dramatic gesture. "When people come into my house and start airing their dirty laundry—"

"This was your stupid idea, not mine!"

"After you told me what the hell you'd pulled, I figured you needed all the help you could get."

Ivy, who'd been merely an observer since dropping her bombshell, announced, "I'm leaving." She set her wineglass on a table and picked up her purse. "My mind is made up. The three of you can debate this till the cows come home, for all I care. You're wasting your time, but it's nothing to me."

"Ivy!" Jack stepped into her path, blocking her speedy exit with his body. His hands itched to grab her, not in violence but because it seemed like a lifetime since he'd held her in his arms. Jeez, he loved this woman! Why couldn't she believe that?

"Get out of my way, Jack."

"Don't do this. You know you don't want to."

How sad she suddenly looked. "That's right, I don't," she admitted. "I don't want to feel the *need* to do it. But it's either this or we say goodbye right here and right now. I simply can't live with a man whose clay feet extend all the way up to his—"

"Ivy!" Cathy wrung her hands anxiously. "I can't believe this is happening. You and Jack are such a perfect couple."

"I thought so, too. Once." The look Ivy gave Jack cut to the bone.

"But—" Cathy looked at her own husband, her usually clear brow knit. "If it can happen to you two, it can happen to anyone."

"Hold on a minute," Rob blustered. "Just because Jack's out running around—"

"Jeez!" Jack let out his breath on a sharp grunt. "With friends like you—"

"You know what I mean," Rob muttered. "Cathy—"

"Get away from me, you . . . you *man!*"

"Goodbye," Ivy announced. "Don't call me, I'll call you—when I get back from my cruise."

"You are *not* going to sleep with another man!" Jack roared. "I won't stand for it! It's—it's a damned barbaric idea—"

"And there's not a thing you can do to stop me," she said softly. "Bon voyage, all. I'm off to find out if infidelity's all it's cracked up to be."

Jack could only watch her go.

JACK CALLED the next day but Ivy, who was screening her calls, refused to pick up the telephone even after hearing his long and impassioned declaration of love and innocence. The next day he came by and pounded on the front door for a good fifteen minutes before giving it up as a lost cause.

The next day she heard nothing from him, which was irritating in the extreme. She'd never expected him to give up this easily, and the fact that he apparently *had* annoyed her considerably. But he'd call or come by tomorrow, she was sure of it. He wasn't about to let her sail away into the arms of another man.

Or was he? He made no further attempts to see her or speak to her for the next four days. On the fifth day, a Sunday, she boarded an airplane at DFW and soared away to San Juan, Puerto Rico, where the *Inamorata II* awaited.

She'd never been to Puerto Rico, or indeed, to the Caribbean. She and Jack, the louse, had planned this trip for years, and now she was taking it alone. With every passing moment, her mood became more morose. By the time the plane landed she was in a positive snit.

The cruise line had sent an open bus and greeters to shepherd passengers through the airport and carry them to the harbor where the ship awaited. Big and white and gleaming, the *Inamorata II* lay at anchor beside the dock, looking just as Ivy had pictured it.

What she hadn't expected was how abandoned she'd feel, being all alone, swept this way and that by a crowd that was at once eager and anxious and, occasionally, downright rude. When at last she started up the gangplank, an elderly woman with silver hair shoved past, knocking Ivy against the rope guardrail.

She was steadied by a pair of helping hands and found herself looking up into the face of an incredibly handsome man of perhaps fifty. He smiled, fine creases appearing around eyes as blue as Paul Newman's.

"Thank you," she gasped, regaining her balance. "My goodness, that lady almost knocked me overboard and I'm not even on the ship yet."

"Use of the word *lady* may be a stretch," he said in a fine drawl that spoke of Virginia. "Are you all right now?"

Ivy returned his smile, grateful for the first personal contact she'd had since climbing on the plane in Dallas. "I'm fine," she said. "I just hope this isn't a portent of things to come."

"Surely not." He touched her elbow lightly to guide her toward the ship's officer waiting at the top to welcome them aboard. Stepping through behind her onto the ship, the stranger gave her a brief and graceful salute with his left hand before disappearing into the crowd.

She wished he'd stayed longer. He might be nearly old enough to be her father but he had a courtly, elegant charm that she found enormously appealing.

It took her half an hour or so to locate her cabin on C Deck. Opening the door with the card key, she walked inside and stopped short, looking around with quick appreciation.

What a lovely room! Royal blue wall-to-wall carpet covered the floor, and the gold spread on the queen-size bed matched heavy drapes swathing a picture window at the far end of the room—not a round porthole as she'd naively expected but a true window.

Everything was compact, not cramped, arranged to take advantage of every inch of space. Theatrical lighting on a mirrored wall to the left of the entry, above a vanity, was a nice touch, she thought.

And so was the enormous bouquet of red sweetheart roses on the table between the bed and a curving couch which circled one side of the small room. She grimaced; had she and Jack told the cruise line they were honeymooners or was this possibly a Valentine's perk?

Then she saw the basket of fruit on the counter. It seemed unlikely that all passengers received such tokens. And she was sure the bottle of champagne in an ice bucket beside the fruit wasn't standard.

Suspicious now, she went over to smell the roses, but there was little to smell. Hothouse posies; they just weren't the same. She plucked a card from a plastic holder nestled among the stems.

Opening the card, she read, "Yes, it's me—and I still love you, no matter what—" With an exclamation of displeasure, she tossed the card aside. Nuts! Jack had made his own bed and now he could lie in it—alone, or maybe not.

A discreet knock on the door brought her swinging around. A smiling black steward stood in the hallway, surrounded by her bags.

"Your luggage, m'lady," he said with a charming Caribbean lilt. His teeth flashed a brilliant white in his dark face. "I'm Des*mond,* here to serve you. May I bring your luggage inside, m'lady? May I open your champagne?" He glanced around with a frown. "Where's your mister? He's not here yet? Maybe you wanna save th' champagne."

"Not a chance." She gestured him in. "I think I'd like to have you open the bottle right now. You see…" She watched him expertly stack the luggage and turn to the wine cooling on the table. "I'll be sailing alone so what's the point of saving anything?"

Anything at all.

Ivy STOOD near a glass wall in the Lovebird Bar, looking out over the sparkling lights of San Juan. The ship was due to get under way at ten o'clock. For some reason, she found herself holding her breath in anticipation.

She was going to do this; she was really going to do this, she told herself for the hundredth time. Vengeance would be hers. She took another sip of her drink, seeking courage however false.

One of the white-coated waiters approached. "Another drink, m'lady?" He grinned. "That mango cooler's not bad, huh?"

"Not bad at all," she agreed. The waiter who'd brought it to her had explained that the drink in the tall, curved glass contained rum, mango, orange and lemon juices and other good things. All she knew was that it was a lovely shade of coral and tasted like party punch. "Sure," she decided. "I'll have another."

"Comin' right up, m'lady." With a slight bow, he backed away, holding his small tray high.

A velvety voice spoke from behind her. "I thought I saw you in the buffet line earlier, but I was too far away to get your attention."

She was already smiling when she turned to find her recent benefactor, the handsome gentleman who'd assisted her earlier, smiling at her. "Hello! I was hoping I'd see you again."

"It was inevitable, considering this is a ship." He returned her smile. "I'm Mitchell Kerr, by the way."

"Ivy Conrad."

He glanced around. "You can't be sailing alone?"

She sighed, feeling sorry for herself. "I'm afraid so. You?"

A brief shadow crossed his face. "Also alone, unfortunately."

"Have you cruised before?" she asked. "I have to admit I'm beginning to wonder if it was wise of me to come alone after—"

His blue eyes narrowed shrewdly but he didn't ask the obvious. "I've cruised many times, but this is the first time I've tried it alone. I'm not terribly concerned about being lonely, however, nor should you be. There are many things to see and do, many new and interesting people to meet—present company not excluded."

Before she could respond, the waiter appeared with her mango cooler and a much more serious-looking drink for Mitchell.

"Scotch and soda," he explained, waving off her attempt to offer her plastic cruise card to pay for her drink and presenting his own instead. "I'm of the old school which says a drink should taste like a drink, not soda pop."

"Yah, mon," the waiter concurred with a broad white grin in Ivy's direction. "'Cept for pretty ladies, of course."

"Of course." Transaction completed, Mitchell turned back to his companion. "Would you care to join me for a stroll around the deck in anticipation of our imminent departure?"

"I'd love to," she said sincerely, suddenly feeling much more optimistic about this adventure.

THEY STROLLED SLOWLY around the gleaming hardwood deck, drinks in hand, talking quietly while getting to know each other. Mitchell was a former public relations executive from New York City by way of Arlington, Virginia. He was also obviously quite well-off, for his cabin was definitely in the high-rent district of the ship—one floor above Ivy's on B Deck—a suite, actually.

A suite he'd inhabited many times with his wife. When he spoke of her, his face took on a distant sadness that tore at Ivy's heart.

"I lost her almost two years ago, shortly after our last cruise together," he explained softly. Leaning his elbows against the polished wooden rail, he spoke with a perfect composure that failed to conceal the depth of his feelings. "It's been difficult since then. I thought perhaps if I revisited the ship, even alone, I might somehow..." He sighed. "It's childish, I suppose. But my daughter encouraged me, so here I am."

Ivy touched his arm lightly, hoping to offer support. "It's beautiful, actually. You must have loved your wife very much." Unlike some husbands she could name.

"Yes." Mitchell drew a quick breath and straightened. "And what about you? Why is a beautiful married lady such as yourself—"

"Married! How did you—" But then she knew; like an idiot, she'd forgotten to remove her wedding ring. Which she quickly remedied, tugging it from her finger and thrusting it into the pocket of her white linen trousers.

"Ah," Mitchell said. "So that's how it is."

She nodded. "When we booked this cruise, my husband and I planned a second honeymoon to celebrate our seventh wedding anniversary on Valentine's Day. But something...happened. Rather than cancel, I decided—" She eyed him warily. This was not the time to bare her soul, she decided.

"You came alone," he finished for her, as if it were a perfectly natural thing to do. "Well, why not? I suppose you need breathing room, time to think. You can certainly get that here."

"Yes, but I'm not sure that's why I came. I had plenty of time to think in Dallas—too much, actually."

"And your husband? If you came alone on the cruise, where is he?"

"I don't know. Back in Texas, I suppose. Or maybe he's working. He's a pilot." She looked around at people strolling past, at others just coming through a door onto the deck—and did a double take. "Or maybe he's stabbed me in the back," she gasped. Gripping Mitchell's arm, she pointed toward the apparition strolling toward them.

Jack Conrad in the flesh: tall, tanned and terrific. He looked from right to left and back again; obviously he hadn't spotted her yet. Reacting to panic, she crouched, hanging on to Mitchell's arm and keeping her head down.

"Don't let him see me!" she begged.

"Who? Is that your husband?" Mitchell looked around. "But, Ivy, this is a ship! You can't hide from him forever."

"I can try. Here, I'm going to stand up and walk the other way very calmly, and I want you to please, *please* walk right behind me. I'll duck into the nearest door, okay? Please, Mitchell! I'll be forever in your debt."

She stood up and took a hasty step in the opposite direction, her wide-eyed gaze seeking a path through the groups of passengers streaming out to enjoy the sailing.

And who should she see approaching from that direction, with a broad grin on his face, but Bart Van Horn, handsome land developer Bart Van Horn, handsome *horny* land developer Bart Van Horn of Florida fame.

JACK DIDN'T KNOW exactly what kind of reception to expect from Ivy but definitely not the one he got: none. She was too busy hugging the tall guy with the mustache to—

Who the hell was the tall guy with the mustache?

For that matter, who the hell was the old guy with the graying blond hair, hauling Ivy out of the other guy's arms with a shocked, "Here, here, that'll be enough of that!"?

Jack had to agree. "Damn straight," he said, reaching the trio at that moment. "Ivy, you've got some explaining to do!"

Her cheeks were flushed, and her beautiful blue eyes were evasive. "Go away, Jack."

The one with the mustache frowned at the old guy. "Who," he said, "are *you?*"

The old guy didn't give an inch. "I'm a friend of this young lady's," he said in a classy Southern accent. "I do not believe she welcomed your advances."

"Neither did I," Jack butted in. "Ivy, who are these guys and why are you runnin' around this cruise ship with 'em?"

Mustache said, "Ivy, aren't you glad to see me?"

And Gray Hair added, "If you'd like me to call for assistance, Ivy—"

And Ivy put her hands over her ears and said, "Will you all just shut up for a minute!"

They did, all three of them standing there expectantly waiting for her to take charge. When it became apparent that she was too stunned...or confused...or too *something* to do so, the old guy cleared his throat.

"I," he said with dignity, "am a recent acquaintance of Miss—"

"Mrs." Jack made the correction automatically, glowering at the man.

Who dipped his head in polite acknowledgment. "—of Ivy's. My name is Mitchell Kerr."

He offered his hand to Jack, who took it somewhat reluctantly.

"I'm Jack Conrad, Ivy's husband." He bit down hard on the last word. "That is, Ivy's my *wife*."

"Estranged wife." Ivy finally found her voice.

Jack was too ticked to exercise caution. He glared at Mustache. "Whatever. We're married."

Mustache grinned. "Jake. Of course." He offered his hand. "I'd know you anywhere. Joan's told me all about you."

Jack frowned. "Joan?"

Ivy gritted her teeth. "Your mother-in-law, turkey."

Jack suppressed a groan. "Oh, that Joan." He shook hands with Mustache, realizing only belatedly that the guy had called him Jake. "That's Jack, by the way."

"Really? I'd have sworn Joan called you—" He shrugged. "Never mind what Joan called you. I'm Bart Van Horn. I'm a land developer in Florida, where

I recently had the pleasure of meeting your lovely wife.''

This was getting way too complicated. Jack thought out loud: "You mean you just *happened* to meet Ivy while she was helping out her mother, and now you just *happen* to find yourself on the same cruise ship with her?"

Van Horn raised his brows, looking way too satisfied. "Quite a coincidence, isn't it. Ivy—"

But Ivy ignored him; she was too busy glaring at Jack as if she'd just come out of a trance. "Okay, we're all introduced. Now do you want to tell me what you think you're doing here, Jack Conrad?"

"Uh . . ." Jack glanced a warning toward the other two men. "Don't you think we should discuss this privately, Ivy?"

"We have nothing to discuss, privately or otherwise. You're not supposed to be here. Get off this ship!"

"But, Ivy—"

"I mean now!"

"I've already paid and—"

"I will not—repeat, *will not* let you into my cabin and that is final."

"Sweetheart, darling, you can't mean—"

"Oh, no?" She lifted her left hand and wiggled her naked ring finger at him. "See this?"

He recoiled in horror. "Where's your wedding ring?"

"Off! It's off and it's staying off until after I—"

"Don't say it!"

Mustache beamed. "No wedding ring. This is very, very interesting. Joan didn't tell me it was this seri—"

"Joan!" In unison, Ivy and Jack turned on him.

"My goodness," Mitchell Kerr interrupted, unbelievably gracious despite all the goings-on around him. "I do believe the ship is under way."

And so it was. Whether or not Ivy was going to let Jack into her cabin and her bed, she definitely wasn't going to get him off her ship.

Not right away, anyhow.

5

WHEN IVY SAID she wouldn't let Jack into her cabin, she wasn't just whistling "Dixie." She literally slammed the door in his face. Even knowing what was bound to come next, he waited.

His expectations did not go unfulfilled. A woman who would pile all his stuff in the driveway and toss a match on it certainly wouldn't hesitate to pitch all his other stuff out into the passageway of a plush cruise ship. Sure enough, the door opened minutes later just long enough for his flight bag to fly out. His suitcase quickly followed.

His shaving kit, which he'd optimistically opened in the bathroom, made its exit last, barely missing his head.

Desmond, the steward, approaching down the passageway, stopped short. "Ah, mon, you be in big trouble," he declared mournfully.

Jack began gathering up his stuff. "You got that right," he agreed glumly.

Desmond knelt and took the leather shaving kit from Jack's hands to finish the job. "Where you gonna sleep, mon?" he asked in a worried tone. "M'lady don't act like she's in no mood t' be reasonable."

"You noticed that, huh." Jack sat back on his heels, bent arms on his thighs, feeling like a complete idiot.

And then he remembered his ace in the hole. "There might be one possibility," he said, thinking out loud.

"Yah, mon?"

"I understand Rusti Wheeler is the entertainment on this cruise."

Desmond let out his breath on a soft, impressed note. "That Rusti, she be som'ting. You know that lady for sure, mon?"

"I went to school with her," Jack said, "but I haven't seen her in years. A mutual friend ran into her on a cruise a while back. I'm not sure she'd even remember me, but if she did, she might come up with something to help me out. Rusti was never lacking in ideas, back in the old days." Which was an understatement.

"Then you in luck, mon. She come on board in San Juan and Desmond's about to show you where to find th' lady." He nodded enthusiastically, as if Jack's problem had been solved.

IVY'S BED was comfortable, her cabin pleasant, the scene through her window a soothing stretch of sea and starlit sky.

If she hadn't been so furious she'd probably have enjoyed herself. Unfortunately, Jack's unexpected appearance had thrown her for a loop.

What in the world did he mean, showing up that way? Did he honestly think she'd take him in and all would be forgiven?

And Bart—what was he doing here? The presence of the two men really threw a monkey wrench into her plans. She was here to find a lover for a one-night stand. How was she going to do that with Jack hovering in the background and Bart hanging around trying to volunteer?

Her mother was going to get an earful, Ivy thought wrathfully. She leaned her elbows on the wide windowsill and stared out at the mysterious sea.

Only Mitchell escaped her wrathful thoughts. What a fine gentleman he was. She was sure he'd make an equally fine friend. Why, if he was fifteen years younger... even ten—

Smiling at last, she slipped into the big bed and eventually drifted off into a restless sleep. She awoke the next morning with plenty of time to prepare for her eight forty-five sitting for breakfast. A long, leisurely shower made her feel better; so did slipping into a cotton sundress she'd chosen especially for this cruise.

She smoothed the flowered fabric over her hips, thinking that Jack had never seen this dress. In fact, he hadn't seen any of her new clothes. She really had thought of this as a second honeymoon and had planned to surprise him... in a multitude of ways.

Her pleasant mood evaporated. Somebody had been surprised, all right, but it hadn't been Jack.

THE HALL OUTSIDE the main dining room was wall-to-wall people by the time she arrived. Hanging back to avoid the crush, she looked around cautiously, but saw neither Jack nor Bart, to her vast relief.

Despite her best efforts, she couldn't help wondering where Jack had spent the night. Under a table somewhere, she devoutly hoped. Idly she wondered if they could throw you off a boat as a stowaway if they kept catching you sleeping in unauthorized places.

She hoped.

The mob moved forward at a snail's pace. Once inside the door, she paused to look around, uncertain which way she should turn. A smiling waiter approached.

Returning his smile, she handed him her seating card. He glanced at it, then looked again more carefully.

"Your seating assignment has been changed, madame," he said in an accent so faint she couldn't place it. "If I may escort you—"

With a slight bow, he gestured her to one side of the huge room, toward the windows. Threading her way between tables large and small, she'd reached her own before she realized who awaited her there.

Three men, actually, and all three stood at her approach.

She planted her hands on her hips. "I don't believe this," she muttered. She turned on the hapless waiter. "There's been some mistake. I don't want to sit here. Take me to my original table, please."

He looked aghast. "Madame, your husband said—"

"I'm not speaking to my husband." She kept her gaze glued to the waiter. "Anything he may say is completely beside the point."

"Ah, so. But the other gentleman, Mr. Van Horn, said that—"

"I'm not speaking to Mr. Van Horn, either."

The waiter appeared horrified. "Then Mr. Kerr—madame, Mr. Kerr is one of the finest men ever to sail aboard this cruise ship. He assured me that you would be pleased to join him at his table."

Ivy risked a glance at Mitchell. He gave her a shrug with lifted brows as if to say, "I meant well!"

"I'm always pleased to join Mr. Kerr," she conceded. "But those other two—get them out of here. Can you do that?"

"Ah, madame." The waiter sighed dramatically. "All seating assignments have been made. If you insist, of course, I shall do my best. It will cause me untold trouble—I may even lose my job, but of course, you have your rights as a passenger. I am here only to serve at your pleasure. If you really cannot stand to break bread with these gentlemen—"

"All right, all right, I get the picture." Ivy gave in and gave up with a sigh of exasperation. "If you're absolutely certain there's no way—"

"I am, I am! Thank you, madame! Thank you, thank you, thank you."

The waiter pulled out her chair. Still she hesitated, knowing she really didn't want to be here, but she was reluctant to make a scene to make a point. She also realized that sea air—or something—had given her a hearty appetite. Outmaneuvered, she sat down and let the waiter unfold a snowy linen napkin and drop it into her lap.

Only then did she address the only man here whose opinion mattered to her. "Mitchell," she said, "I'd expect this kind of thing from Jack and Bart, but *you?*"

Mitchell gave her a whimsical shrug. "I fear I've disappointed you, but my intentions were the best. I did request that we share a table, inasmuch as I find you pleasant company. Since I'm a longtime and faithful cruiser on this ship, I am granted certain privileges. These gentlemen—" he gestured toward the hitherto silent duo "—will have to speak for themselves."

She turned on Jack. "So?"

He looked well pleased with himself, not to mention well rested—darn it. "Husbands are usually seated with wives, that is, if they want to be."

"Oh, brother!" She addressed Bart in the same unforgiving tone. "And you?"

"Simple," he said, looking just as smug as Jack had. "I told the maître d' we were lovers."

"You *what?*" Ivy gasped.

"You *what?*" Jack surged from his chair like a bull elk emerging from the forest.

"Just joking." Bart did not appear daunted. "I slipped him ten bucks. It was simple."

Everything else about this cruise, apparently, was going to be complicated.

BREAKFAST on the *Inamorata II* was an affair to remember. Dining in elegant surroundings beneath glittering chandeliers, at tables draped and decked with fine linen and crystal and china, served by solicitous waiters and bus persons, the meal proceeded with leisurely excess.

Name it and it was instantly available. Juices covered the spectrum, as did fresh fruits. Trays passed by loaded with doughnuts, Danish, croissants, brioche, muffins, biscuits, sweet rolls, bagels, toast. Eggs came boiled, fried, basted, poached, scrambled, omeleted or imitation; accompaniments included bacon, ham, sausages link and patty, corned beef hash and steak. Grits or hash browns? One need but ask.

And then there were the specialties: eggs Benedict covered with delicate hollandaise, pancakes plain or with bananas or raisins or pecans or all three, French toast or Scottish kippers or finnan haddie, smoked salmon with cream cheese or marinated herring.

"Look, Ivy," Jack said, pointing to the menu. "Your favorite."

Yes, eggs Benedict was a weakness of hers, but she'd be damned if she'd let him anticipate her that way.

She had a veggie omelet just to spite him and found it so delicious she couldn't be sorry. She also had a bowl of fresh strawberries and cream and just one little bran muffin.

All three men ate heartily, putting aside their differences out of respect for a fabulous meal. As always, the wait staff hovered unobtrusively in the background, refilling coffee cups and water glasses, whisking away plates to fetch fresh ones filled with yet another delicacy. At last Ivy placed her hand over her coffee cup to signal she'd reached satiety.

"Good grief," she groaned, "how could anyone spend more than a few days on one of these boats without gaining a ton? I'm barely past breakfast and already I'm in troub—"

"Yoo-hoo! Jackie, yoo-hoo!"

The light, feminine voice cut through Ivy's inane chatter. Looking around, she saw a woman approaching; rephrase that. A *gorgeous* woman approaching. The newcomer was tall and redheaded, and she looked like a showgirl.

This beautiful creature paused behind Jack's chair. Putting her hands on his shoulders, she smiled around the table. "Hi, all," she said cheerfully. "I'm a friend of Jackie's."

"Jackie?" Ivy choked on a sip of water and dived for her napkin.

Jack looked...not exactly uncomfortable; more like defiant. *"Old* friend," he reiterated. "We went to school together in Corpus Christi. Anybody got a problem with that?"

Bart looked more than interested. "Not me," he said. "I'm Bart Van Horn."

The redhead kept right on smiling. "I'm Rusti Wheeler."

"I'm Ivy Conrad."

"I guessed." Rusti grinned at Ivy.

"I'm Jackie's wife."

"I guessed that, too."

"I should have said *estranged* wife. Or maybe you guessed that, too."

"Didn't have to guess. I already knew it."

Jack looked distinctly uneasy. "Rusti's with a dance troupe," he explained. "She'll be entertaining at Sweethearts Show Room tonight."

"I'll bet she's very good at what she does," Ivy said sweetly.

Rusti laughed out loud. "I sure am." She winked at Ivy, then expanded her attention to include them all. "I just dropped by to meet Jackie's friends and invite you all to my exercise class at eleven on A Deck. It's the only way to enjoy yourself on a cruise ship without packing on the pounds."

With a quick wave of one graceful hand, she turned to weave her way back through the tables. Every male whose line of vision she crossed reacted as if she were a magnet in bright yellow—and did she ever enjoy it!

Ivy glared at Jack, who was probably the only man in the room over the age of twelve who wasn't watching the dancer's exit. Her guess was, he'd already seen everything there was to see.

"So," she said before she could stop herself, "where did *you* spend the night, or need I ask?"

"Where do you think?" he shot back.

Ivy lifted her chin. "Where do you think I think?"

"Where do you think I think you think?"

"Children!" Mitchell leaned forward, including them both in his smiling disapproval. "This is getting you nowhere. If you'd just be honest with each other, I'm sure you could—"

"I honestly don't think so." Ivy stood up, tossing her napkin on the table. "*Jackie's* perfectly free to sleep anywhere he wants to. And so am I!"

With her head held high, she turned and followed Rusti's path out of the dining room.

THE SHIP, Ivy soon discovered, was a world unto itself. With seven public decks and who knew how many more below that were off-limits to guests, it offered a mind-boggling variety of things to see and do.

It took considerable effort, but she finally managed to slip away from the Terrible Trio to explore on her own. She began at the very top on the A Deck, intending to work her way down. There she found the spa and sauna, a complete beauty salon and several

shops offering everything from toothpaste to dia-
mond rings, all duty free.

The A Deck also boasted a swimming pool, heart-
shaped and surrounded by lounge chairs. At mid-
morning, most of the chairs were already occupied by
sun worshipers, while a few more-athletic souls frolicked in the azure water. At the very end of the deck—
"aft," a passing waiter had supplied; the pointy end
was "fore"—a full bar offered food and drink.

Rusti came hustling up the stairwell just as Ivy pre-
pared to go down. The redhead, looking pleased,
called a greeting. "Comin' to my exercise class?" she
inquired.

Ivy was about to state a definitive "No!" but
stopped before uttering the word. Why not? Obviously, she was going to need help if she hoped to still
fit into her clothes at the end of this cruise.

"Maybe," she said without much enthusiasm.

"Great!" Rusti looked totally delighted. She also
looked totally fantastic in tight white shorts that flattered her long, tanned legs. And the equally tight white
T-shirt didn't do her any damage, either. "See you
later, then! Half hour—don't be late!"

She trotted away toward a cleared area on the shin-
ing hardwood deck. After a quick look around, she
proceeded on inside through a door marked Crew
Only.

Ivy reconsidered. Did she really want to get all hot
and sweaty with her husband's latest squeeze?

Just then Jack appeared at the top of the stairs. He
apparently didn't even notice his *wife* standing off to
one side. No, he just strode right on past to disappear
through the same door Rusti had taken.

Ivy scowled after him. On second thought, she decided, she owed it to herself to at least *try* to keep in shape.

SHE'D DASHED to her cabin to don red shorts and a navy blue T-shirt, white sneakers and a white terry headband to keep her shaggy-cut blond hair out of her face. At Rusti's command, Ivy lined up in ragged array with the rest of the class.

She was as ready as she'd ever be.

Breathing deeply of the fresh sea air, she was suddenly glad she'd decided to do this. All at once she felt great, full of energy.

Too much energy, she admitted to herself: it needed release. She began the warm-up stretching in imitation of their leader. To one side, a pudgy woman in pedal pushers and horizontally striped T-shirt puffed and panted in time; on the other, a bored-looking teen wearing headphones pretended to go through the motions.

Too much energy, Ivy thought again—sexual energy she could have been expending on the ungrateful wretch she'd married. But since he'd forfeited all rights in that department, she was faced with finding a substitute so she could teach her husband a richly deserved lesson.

At the rate he was going, though, there might not be enough men on board this tub to even the score.

"Okay," Rusti cried in ringing tones, "turn to your right and march in place."

Ivy followed instructions, hands on her hips and shoulders back. Was she jumping to conclusions or had Jack really slept with Rusti last night? And what about—

"Another right turn, and keep those knees high!" Rusti commanded.

Ivy obeyed and came face-to-face with Bart Van Horn, who was grinning at her although he should have turned in another direction. He winked, then pivoted smartly.

At which point she saw that Jack occupied the slot directly behind Bart. Jack didn't wink; he didn't even smile. He simply locked his gaze with hers for a long, meaningful moment before turning in the appropriate direction.

And when he did, Mitchell Kerr leaned slightly to one side and gave her a little wave.

So her watchdogs had tracked her down, she thought, marching in place while dragging in deep breaths of fresh and invigorating sea air. *Damn.* The way they were shadowing her she wouldn't be able to accomplish her clandestine purpose even if she tried.

Did she want to? Did she really? If she did, all she had to do was crook her little finger at Bart and it would be a done deal. But while she'd found him attractive in Florida, he seemed so much less desirable now. She wondered why.

Because of Jack, she decided, making another quarter turn at Rusti's command. Because, although she'd been a little tempted in Florida, there'd never been any real chance that she would be unfaithful. She'd enjoyed the attention and the brief flirtation; it had been enough to fill her with a pleasurable guilt and a needed reassurance that despite nearly seven years of marriage, she was still a desirable woman.

"Okay, folks!" Rusti clapped her hands for the attention of the perspiring exercisers. She, herself, looked just as cool and gorgeous as when they'd congregated beneath the blazing Caribbean sun.

"Now that we're all warmed up," she said in an unrelentingly cheerful voice, "I'm going to lead you through a few aerobic exercises. Those who'd prefer to jog, follow the yellow line around the deck, keeping to the outside so you don't mow down any slowpokes. The rest of you follow along...three steps left, kick—swing those arms, swing those arms! Three steps right—"

Not a chance, Ivy quickly decided; she'd leave them all in the dust and jog away to confront her thoughts in solitude. Stepping out of line, she hastened to the rail where the yellow line pointed the way.

Bart followed; after a moment's hesitation, Jack followed Bart. On completion of their first pass around the ship, Mitchell stepped out of the crowd and fell into line at the end.

For the next forty minutes, Ivy led her little band of intrepid runners around and around the uppermost deck of the *Inamorata II,* her knees pumping high and her eyes straight ahead.

Only her thoughts kept turning back.

6

BEING PART OF A QUARTET got old fast for Ivy. By the second day at sea she was already tired of matching wits with her table companions and decided to skip lunch in the dining room.

One thing this cruise ship had was food: food everywhere, from breakfast to afternoon teas to midnight buffets and complete room service. She'd never even miss lunch.

Unfortunately, not even the *Inamorata II* offered *man* service. She'd have liked to just ring up, order a healthy specimen of male pulchritude and get it over with. Plus, being under almost constant scrutiny by the troublesome trio was not doing her nerves a lot of good.

Taking the last available table beneath a brightly striped red-and-white canopy at three that afternoon, she placed two overflowing plates before her with a sigh of surrender. She shouldn't, she really shouldn't...but she couldn't resist what the beautiful poolside buffet offered.

One plate held the healthy stuff: salads, both fruit and vegetable. The other plate contained an enormous cheeseburger, and big planks of golden French-fried potatoes. Both were favorites in which she rarely allowed herself to indulge.

She'd hate herself in the morning....

A smiling waiter delivered a tall glass of sparkling-clear iced tea. She murmured her thanks, then picked up her fork to take that first heavenly bite of luscious fresh papaya. Savoring the fruit, she looked around at her fellow revelers—and realized with a start that she was the only person dining alone.

Feeling like a social outcast, she decided she'd just have to do something about that. She'd invite the first unattached man she spotted to join her, that's what she'd do.

Wandering into view came a couple, not a lone stranger. Young and attractive, they paused uncertainly, balancing plates and silverware and looking around without much hope of finding a place to light.

What the heck. Ivy smiled and gestured to them. "I've got plenty of room at my table," she said, stating the obvious. "If you'd care to join me...?"

The woman smiled and glanced at her companion. The man nodded and placed his plate and silver on the table before turning to pull out her chair.

"Thanks," he said cheerfully, sitting down himself. "I'm Kevin Phillips and this is Jill—" He broke up with laughter. "I almost said Jill Crane but it's Jill Phillips now. We were married three days ago in Palm Beach."

A becoming blush touched Jill's cheeks. "We're on our honeymoon," she said softly, reaching out to stroke Kevin's hand where it lay on the table. She glowed with that special connection enjoyed only by the young and naive.

Great, Ivy thought, struggling to keep her own smile firmly in place. Honeymooners. *Just what I need.*

"I'm Ivy Conrad," she said. "I'm delighted to meet you."

"Thanks," they said in unison. "Happy to meet you."

Kevin picked up a grape from his overflowing plate and offered it to his bride. Jill took it into her mouth with a deliberation which made Ivy feel faint, not to mention salacious. She cleared her throat and tried to look away, without much success.

Jill licked her lips. "We've noticed you before," she said to Ivy. "For one thing, I love your wardrobe." She selected a morsel of melon and popped it into her husband's mouth. "And then there's your fan club."

"My—?" Good grief, were they making a spectacle of themselves? "Oh, them." Ivy shrugged. "I haven't the faintest idea why they insist on following me around."

"No?" Jill looked amused. "I get the idea they don't want to let you out of their collective sight. Now that I think about it, this is the first time I've seen you without one or all of them in attendance."

Ivy grimaced. "I'm surprised you even noticed...unless we're disturbing the other passengers?"

"Not at all." Kevin took his wife's hand and kissed her palm, making her shiver. "We noticed because we have a table not far from yours in the dining room." He nibbled at Jill's fingers. "A table for two."

"How nice." Ivy chewed on her bottom lip. "I'm afraid I *didn't* notice." Actually, she hadn't noticed anyone or anything except her three—she'd almost thought of them as *suitors*.

"Why would you?" Jill laughed. "With three handsome men competing for your attention—"

"You think they're handsome?" Kevin frowned.

His new wife patted his cheek. "Not as handsome as you," she assured him. "And no way near as sexy."

"That's more like it."

Good grief, Ivy thought; they looked as if they were about to...do something *impetuous* right here on good old A Deck.

"So tell me," she interjected quickly, "are you from Florida or did you just go there to get married? I'm from Dallas—"

Jill and Kevin pried themselves apart long enough to answer her. Then apparently hunger—for food, this time—got to Kevin and he turned to his plate with the appetite of a starving man. Jill humored him, answering Ivy's questions and asking her own. Slowly the steamy atmosphere cooled off a few degrees.

But the sexual vibrations between the newlyweds remained palpable, making Ivy both envious and resentful.

This was supposed to be *her* honeymoon, too. Life simply wasn't fair and she deeply resented it.

ONE THING meeting the Phillipses did was spur Ivy on in her resolve. She'd come on this cruise for a reason, and she was going to see it through no matter what.

Dressing early for the second seating at dinner, she went down two decks to one of the many lounges. It was nearly deserted at 7:00 p.m.; those with first seating at dinner and most everyone else, apparently, must still be dressing or...otherwise occupied. Thoughts of Jill and Kevin flashed through Ivy's mind.

She ordered a Blue Monday, which was yesterday's special, consisting of blue curaçao, rum and lemon juice. She figured it would doubtless taste just as good on a Tuesday. Choosing a small table near the windows so she could admire the view, she sat down to wait.

This was not going the way she'd hoped—not too surprising, since Jack hadn't been part of the plan. Neither had Bart; her mother was going to hear about this. Ivy was thankful that at least she hadn't confided her plan to her blabbermouth parent, so Bart didn't know what she was really up to.

Suddenly she felt a burning need to confide in someone, anyone. Even surrounded by all these people, she felt so horribly alone. But that didn't stop her from glancing around and considering the possibilities for infidelity.

Which were practically nil. Most of the men in the room were with women; those who weren't offered no temptation whatsoever. But she wasn't looking for temptation. It wasn't as if she planned to enjoy this. This was strictly revenge here.

She forced herself to look again.

There was one unattached guy in the entire room. He was leaning over a bar stool and checking out his surroundings even more intently than she was. He was the right age, she realized, probably mid-to-late thirties, and not all that bad-looking . . . if you felt really, really charitable. Nevertheless, he apparently had the requisite number of body parts and all his hair.

Unfortunately for him, he wore the loudest, most obnoxious sport coat she'd ever laid eyes on. It was an almost Hawaiian-looking print, and the shirt he wore beneath the coat was even louder. His trousers were red, his shoes white, his hair long and he had—of all the outdated things—sideburns.

She decided she wasn't that desperate, at least not yet. On the other hand, if she slept with him or someone like him, no one could ever suggest that her motives were anything but pure....

The cocktail waiter delivered the Blue Monday, which Ivy had already dubbed a Blue Tuesday. She offered her cruise card, thinking how nice it was to simply sign for anything she wanted, especially knowing the bill would go to dear old Jack. Maybe tomorrow she'd check out the gift shop.

Settling back in the comfortable barrel-shaped chair, she waited for someone interesting to cross her line of vision. Wouldn't you know, the first appealing male to appear was good old Mitchell Kerr. He spotted her at once and threaded his way through the tables and around the small, empty dance floor to reach her.

Looking at him objectively, she had to admit he really was extraordinarily good-looking, and in excellent shape, too; she knew this because he'd worn shorts and a short-sleeved T-shirt for their daily runs. Mitchell didn't take a back seat to anybody in the looks department, not even Jack. Or Bart. Or Paul Newman or Robert Redford.

"I was hoping to run into you," he said. "May I join you?"

"Please." She gestured toward the empty chair. So what if his presence would doubtless scare away any potential bed mates. As if she could care, considering how slim the pickin's.

He sat. "We missed you at lunch."

She shrugged. "I didn't feel up to another group date."

He laughed. "Is that how it seems to you?"

She glowered. "That's how it *is*. Jack's trying to snow me, Bart's trying to hit on me and you—"

Mitchell raised one brow, waiting.

She softened. "You, I think, are trying to protect me. It's really very nice of you, but I'm a big girl and I don't need a keeper."

"Think not?" He gestured for the waiter to approach. "You should be with your husband, Ivy."

"It's his fault I'm not," she retorted, but his remark had startled her. "Have you spoken to him about this?" she added. And then she had an even more disturbing thought, which she voiced: "You don't, by any chance, know what this is all about, do you?"

"I can make an educated guess." To the waiter, he said, "Scotch and soda." For her benefit, he added, "I haven't been prying, if that's what's worrying you."

She almost wished he would. Mitchell seemed so... nonjudgmental. If she could confide in anyone, it would be him. But not just yet. Maybe after dinner she'd see her chance.

They settled down comfortably to desultory conversation. The minutes slipped past; passengers from the first dinner seating began to drift in. Still Mitchell's drink did not appear. Finally he rose.

"I think it'd be faster if I went to the bar myself,"
he said. "May I bring you another one of those
things?"

Ivy glanced down, surprised to find her glass empty.
"That would be kind of you," she acquiesced.

"Uhh ... what is it?"

"A Blue Monday. Appropriate for any day of the
week."

He went away smiling. As if on cue, a figure stepped
to the side of the table, causing her to look around in
surprise.

It was Mr. Snappy Dresser from the bar. She could
have groaned but settled for a polite but pointed lifting of her brows.

He grinned broadly. Up close his ensemble was even
more hideous.

"Saw you giving me the eye earlier," he said, jerk-
ing his head toward the bar. "Ditch the old guy and
let's make us some beautiful music together." He
winked.

"I beg your pardon?" She looked down her nose at
him.

He remained undeterred. "Hey, I know when a
babe's interested."

"Wrong on both counts. I'm not a *babe,* and I'm
certainly not interested." This guy was a dolt, she realized, but not a scary dolt. She'd refrain from hurting his feelings ... any more than she had to.

His wolfish grin got a little bit wider. "Don't play
hard to get. To know me is to love me, sweet cheeks."

He reached for a chair, only to freeze with his hand
in the air. Ivy's surprised glance lifted to his startled

face and moved on to the hand clamped on his shoulder.

Make that *Jack's* hand, clamped on his shoulder like a vise.

"The lady says *no*," Jack said, his tone threatening. "If that's not good enough for you, *I* say no. If that's still not good enough for you, I'd be glad to offer you convincing reasons to—"

"Hey!" Loud Suit yanked himself away from Jack, brushing ineffectively at his jacket as if it had been spoiled—as if that were possible. "Who the hell do you think you are, buster?"

"I *think* I'm that lady's husband." Jack bit down on the words hard. "I think I'm gonna cut your water off if you ever bother her again."

"Your—? Heh, heh, heh." Laughing weakly, Loud Suit appealed to Ivy for support. "You're not his—no way—you *are?*"

"She are," Jack verified grimly. "If you want to end this cruise in the same shape you started, I'd suggest you stay away from my wife. Do I make myself clear?"

"R-*real* clear." The man took a hasty step back. "Hey, lighten up, man! I didn't mean—" Something in Jack's expression apparently convinced him of the hopelessness of his case. He turned and fled.

"And that goes for all your sleazy friends, too," Jack called after him. He sounded well satisfied with himself, but when he turned toward Ivy, he was scowling. "What the hell's going on here? You're just waiting to get picked up, aren't you?"

"How dare you!" She glanced around quickly to see if anyone had noticed the brewing contretemps.

Several "anyones" had. "Jack, why don't you mind your own business?"

"You are my business." He pulled out a chair and was about to sit down, when Ivy stopped him.

"Don't—"

He hesitated, knees bent, hovering over the chair.

"Don't sit down," she said. "That's Mitchell's chair."

"Mitchell?" He frowned. "But I thought that guy..."

"No, Jack, you didn't think," she said angrily, feeling vindicated. "You rarely do, at least not about me. You just go bulldozing your way through life without paying the least attention to my feelings."

"You can't deny that clown was trying to hit on you."

"I don't. But I deny that I needed some big, strong man to save me. I can take care of myself, in case you've forgotten. I got along without you before I met you—"

"Don't *even* go on."

"Why, Jack." Mitchell approached with a glass in each hand. "Will you join us for a drink before dinner?"

"Sure."

"No!"

Both men looked at Ivy, one with surprise and the other with disappointment.

"Aw, Ivy—"

"Go away, Jack. Just go far away and leave me alone!"

For a moment she thought he would defy her wishes. Then he shrugged. "Okay, Ivy—for now. But this isn't even close to over." He turned and stalked away.

Mitchell sat down and placed the glasses on the table. "Ivy, what's this all about? I don't want to pry, but I'm seeing just enough to be worried about both of you." He glanced after Jack, who was disappearing through the double doors into the passageway. "Your husband doesn't seem a bad sort."

Ivy picked up her Blue Monday and swallowed a hearty gulp. "I used to think the sun rose and set on that man. Fool that I was."

"Obviously, something drastic happened to change your mind so completely." He added hastily, "Not that I'm asking what it was."

"You don't need to ask," she said, coming to a sudden decision. She leaned toward him earnestly. "I've got to talk to someone or I think I'll go crazy. It might as well be you."

Mitchell gave her a wry glance. "Think of me as a maiden aunt, then," he suggested.

That made her laugh. "Not even a maiden uncle."

"I'm flattered."

"You should be." Good grief, was she flirting with him? She pulled such thoughts up short. "Promise you won't say a word about this?" she demanded.

He looked uncomfortable. "I won't, but perhaps you'd better think twice about—"

"I have. Mitchell, I . . . I found Jack in bed with another woman."

He looked totally shocked. "In bed—!"

Ivy nodded. "Practically."

He looked relieved. "That's hardly the same thing," he pointed out, ever reasonable.

"Oh, no? How about this, then. There's a naked blonde in our bed and Jackie is singing his little heart out in the shower." Boy, just let Mitchell justify that!

He actually tried. "Did Jack have an explanation?"

"Well, yeah, sure." She brushed it away. "He had to say something, didn't he? He dredged up some ridiculous story about how this woman followed him home like a puppy dog. He said he thought she'd left when he got into the shower. I mean, come *on!* Did *you* ever have a gorgeous woman follow you home, wait until your back was turned, then yank off all her clothes and jump in your bed?"

"Well, no...."

"I rest my case." She leaned back in her chair and crossed her arms over her chest. "Of course, he wasn't expecting me. I came home early from a visit to my mother, hoping to surprise him. He was surprised, all right, but not as much as I was."

Her lips trembled, and tears sprang to her eyes. She'd thought she was past such an emotional reaction.

Mitchell leaned forward to pat her shoulder, not at all awkwardly as most men would have done. "There, there," he said. "It'll be all right, Ivy."

"No, no, it won't. I'm not sure it ever will be all right again, unless..." She stopped speaking and swallowed hard. Did she dare tell him the rest? He was the only friend she had on board this boat, and if he turned away from her, she didn't know what she'd do.

He picked up on her sudden reticence. "Except what? Is there something Jack can do to make amends?"

"Not Jack." She chewed on her lip. "Me."

"I don't understand." His beautiful blue eyes looked meltingly compassionate.

"Jack's completely destroyed my faith in him," she said, choosing her words slowly and carefully. "I feel . . . rightly or wrongly, that I am morally superior to him now."

He nodded. "I can understand that. But things change. With time . . ."

"Time won't do it."

"Then what will?"

She took a deep breath and looked him square in the eyes. "What's sauce for the goose is sauce for the gander," she said.

"What's sauce . . . ?" He frowned. "I'm afraid I don't understand what you're getting at."

She glanced around quickly to make sure no one was near enough to overhear. Even so, she leaned forward to speak in a low, intent voice. "I came on this cruise determined to even the score by sleeping with another man," she whispered. "Maybe when Jack knows how it feels to be betrayed, we'll have a starting point to talk about reconciliation."

"Or divorce," Mitchell added.

7

IVY SUPPOSED she must have flinched, or maybe even gasped, because Mitchell looked so contrite.

"I'm sorry," he said, "but you must consider all the possible consequences of what you are contemplating."

"I have," she insisted.

"Not if you can look so shocked at the mere mention of the word *divorce*."

"I'm not shocked," she said, but that was a lie. She couldn't imagine life without Jack, in spite of everything. Unfortunately, the way things stood, she couldn't imagine life *with* him, either. "Oh, Mitchell, I'm all mixed up!" she confessed.

"That's obvious, or you wouldn't be considering anything so drastic as a cheap affair."

"That's not exactly how I'd characterize it." Her shoulders slumped. "I've disappointed you."

"Not at all." He rose and offered his hand. "I think it's surprise more than anything."

"Or shock."

"Perhaps. Shall we go in to dinner now?"

"But I want to talk to you about this, explain—"

"Later, Ivy. We'll be late for dinner."

Still she hesitated. "I'm not looking forward to seeing Jack at the table. He made a fool of me a few minutes ago."

"No one can make a fool of you without your permission," Mitchell said. "Come along."

So she did. Bart was already at the table, conferring with the sommelier over the wine list. At their approach, he looked up with a smile. "White wine suit everybody?"

"It suits me," Ivy said. She let Mitchell seat her, but before she could reach for her napkin, a waiter was there to open it with a flourish and place it on her lap.

"The pouilly-fuissé, then," Bart told the sommelier.

Ivy waited until the man had bowed himself away before saying with a degree of pleasure, "Of course, Jack doesn't like white wine. But he doesn't have to drink any, does he?"

Bart reached for his water goblet. "Not a problem. Jack won't be joining us for dinner."

She frowned. "Why not?"

"He said something about grabbing a snack with some of the crew members."

"You mean—" Ivy shut her mouth and grit her teeth before Rusti's name tumbled out. "Never mind. I'm *glad* he won't be here." It was exactly what she'd been hoping for. So why did she feel so out of sorts about it?

She picked up the menu and wished she'd had the strength of character to stay away herself. She only read as far as the broiled lobster tail to know what she wanted, although the go-withs took more thought. She finally settled on fresh fruit cocktail, chilled avocado bisque and a salad of lettuce and chicory with baby shrimp and fresh pineapple.

Dessert was an even more difficult choice, and she vacillated between chocolate éclair and piña colada cake. "Try both, m'lady," the waiter urged, but she managed to resist his evil influence.

They drank Bart's wine, and then Mitchell ordered a second bottle and they drank that, too. Somewhere along the way, Ivy felt herself beginning to relax.

Kevin and Jill stopped by on their way out of the dining room, pausing with arms wrapped around each other's waists. After introductions, Jill smiled at Ivy. "Are you going to the Sweethearts Show Room later? I hear the big revue is really something."

"I hadn't thought about it," Ivy admitted. "Maybe."

"Perhaps we'll see you there, then." They began moving away, still wrapped in each other's arms. "Apparently, Rusti What's-her-name is really good."

Ivy hoped her smile hadn't slipped. When they'd gone, she said to her companions, "Honeymooners."

"Who'd have guessed?" Bart grinned and poured the final drops of wine into her glass. "They seem like nice kids."

"I think so, too."

"Would you like to take in the show, then? I'd be happy to escort you."

Mitchell leaned forward with a charming smile. "Shall we make it a threesome? I've seen it before, and it really is an excellent production."

Well, why not? She assured herself that she wasn't trying to keep an eye on Jack and his dance hall floozy—certainly not. The show was probably very good, and why should she miss it when she was a paying customer, just like everyone else?

Shoot, she wasn't even interested in catching Jack in the act—again. Nor was she trying to justify what she was still determined to do—as if she needed more justification.

"Gentlemen," she said with an expansive smile that included both of them, "I accept your kind offers. The Three Musketeers, that's us. One for all and all for one!"

THE SHOW WAS FABULOUS, their seats less so. Mitchell had warned them that people started staking out the best tables early, but they'd lingered over dinner, then had drinks in one of the lounges. Considering the crowd, they were lucky to find any seats at all, even bad ones with the view half-obscured by a pillar.

Within the first two minutes after the houselights dimmed and the show began, Ivy realized that this was a class production. Rusti was undoubtedly the star in this universe, a star wearing sequins and feathers, high heels and a towering headdress which she maneuvered with ease and grace. Damn.

She was not only gorgeous, but a hell of a dancer to boot. It was enough to make Ivy sick. But where was Jack? She looked around for him until she realized Mitchell was watching her. Turning her head back toward the stage, she forced herself to keep her attention glued there.

"Good show," Bart remarked afterward, while the mob filed out and the three of them sat in their out-of-the-way corner waiting for a clear shot at the door.

"These productions really are as good as anything you'll see in Las Vegas, which is as good as anything you'll see anywhere in the world."

"I have to agree," Ivy said, the words ashes on her tongue.

Mitchell nodded. "My wife loved these shows. She couldn't understand how those girls could dance around on high heels on such a small stage without killing themselves and each other." He laughed. "My wife had a wry sense of humor."

Ivy felt her heart melt. "You had a really happy marriage, didn't you?"

He nodded, a smile tugging at the corners of his well-shaped mouth. "Not perfect, you understand, but basically a wonderful—"

His words faded away, or perhaps she just stopped listening, for at that moment Jack appeared around one edge of the closed velvet curtain.

The SOB had been backstage! Ivy was stunned; she couldn't *believe* it.

Bart stood. "I think the crowd's thinned out enough so we can make our getaway," he said. "What'll it be, Ivy? A drink in one of the lounges? Would you like to try your luck at the casino or see a movie? I think there's a stargazing lecture in a half hour or so, if that's your pleasure."

Her pleasure would be killing her husband. "I think I'd like to look at the stars," she said, picking up her small evening purse from the table. "You'll join us, won't you, Mitchell?"

He hesitated. "Perhaps later," he said. "You two run along."

Ivy felt a little chill of foreboding. She'd never expected him to send her off alone with *Bart,* especially now that he knew her plan. She felt almost betrayed that he would.

Not to mention trapped. There was nothing for it now but to let Bart take her elbow and steer her toward the open doors of the show room.

FROM ACROSS THE BIG ROOM, Jack saw Ivy walk out with Bart Van Horn and there wasn't a thing he could do except gnash his teeth. Damn, she looked good! So far he hadn't recognized a single article of clothing she'd worn, including the royal blue sequined dress she had on tonight.

He probably should have gone in to dinner instead of sulking in the crew's dining room. But he'd heard someone remark that "Absence made the heart grow fonder," and he'd been desperate enough to give it a try.

Actually he hadn't seen much of Ivy since their second-morning run around the ship in tandem with her other admirers. One of whom approached him now.

Mitchell Kerr reached out to shake hands. "Good to see you, Jack. We missed you at dinner."

"*We?*"

The older man shrugged.

"So...uh..." Jack fumbled around for the words. "Did Ivy—did you enjoy the show?"

"Ivy and I both enjoyed the show. Your friend, Miss Wheeler, is really quite talented." Mitchell quirked one brow.

"Yeah," Jack agreed without interest or enthusiasm. He wanted to talk about Ivy, not Rusti.

"Not to mention attractive."

"Yeah, I guess so. Back in high school she was sort of an ugly duckling."

"Is that right?"

Jack nodded. "She was taller than most of the boys, including me, and... Hey, wait a minute." He frowned at the other man. "You didn't really *believe* we went to school together, did you."

"What I believe is of little consequence."

"Meaning Ivy doesn't believe it, either."

"Would you, if she said, for example, that she'd gone to school with Mr. Van Horn?"

"Hell, no!" Jack frowned. "She didn't, did she?"

Mitchell laughed. "Not that I know of. That was only an example."

"Okay, I get it." Jack sighed. "In case it comes up, there's nothing between me and Rusti."

"I believe you," Mitchell said.

That surprised Jack considerably. "Thanks."

"I believe you about *that*."

Jack sucked in his breath. Did that mean Ivy had confided in this stranger about what had happened back in Dallas? Nah, he couldn't believe she'd do that... and yet— "Anything else on your mind?" he asked suspiciously.

Mitchell shrugged. "What's between you and your wife is really none of my business," he said in a level voice. "Whatever problems you may have, you'll have to work out on your own." He glanced toward the door. "I'm not entirely sure Mr. Van Horn agrees with me, however."

"Is that guy making headway with Ivy?"

"Easy, Jack." Mitchell patted the younger man's arm. "You're perhaps not in a strong position to play the wronged husband."

"Maybe not," Jack conceded, "but I can't just stand by and let that clown make a move on the woman I love." He clenched his hands into fists.

"No, indeed," Mitchell agreed. "In fact, were she my wife, I'd probably drop in on the stargazing lecture, which begins—" he glanced at his heavy gold wristwatch "—in about a half hour on A Deck. Just to take a look around, of course."

With a final pat to Jack's arm, Mitchell turned and left the show room.

WITH TIME TO SPARE, Bart and Ivy settled at a table on the top deck, where a steel band performed lively Caribbean music. All around them, their fellow cruisers frolicked: some swimming, some dancing, some partaking of the midnight buffet, which opened at eleven in case anyone couldn't last the extra hours between feasts.

Sipping a glass of Riesling, Ivy stared out over lights reflecting off a calm sea.

"Beautiful, isn't it."

At Bart's amused tone, she cast him a questioning glance. "Yes."

"You've never cruised before?"

She shook her head. "You said you had, as I recall. On this same ship?"

He nodded.

On impulse, she said, "Tell me the truth, Bart. How do you happen to be here when you didn't say a word about a cruise when I was in Florida?"

"Didn't I?" His expression remained bland.

She laughed. "You know you didn't."

His lips twitched in a slight smile. "You're right."

"So how did you get a cabin? We had to make reservations months ago."

"There are usually last-minute cancellations. I was lucky."

She knew she should go ahead and ask if he'd gone to all that trouble for her, but she wasn't sure she wanted to hear the answer. "Are you having fun?"

"Yes, but you're not." He looked at her with a level gaze that made her squirm. "And you're not going to, if you refuse to get into the spirit of the thing."

"I...don't quite know what that means." She turned away from him, looking out over the water again.

"It means, you're either with Jack or you're not. If you try to have it both ways, you're going to have a miserable time."

"Let's don't talk about Jack."

"That's a great idea, but it won't work if you keep thinking about him."

"I'm certainly not—"

"Come on; I know why you agreed to go to the show tonight. It was to see if Jack was there—and he was. You expected to see him, but when you did, it ruined the whole thing for you."

"That's absolutely untrue," she denied staunchly. "I wanted to see the show and I did. And I'm *glad* I did. It was sensational."

"You also saw your husband hanging around another woman, and that wasn't so sensational. Why do you let him get to you that way?"

"I—why, I—" She paused, trying to pull herself together enough to give him a coherent answer, realized she didn't have to explain herself to him and said somewhat indignantly, "I'm not going to confide in you."

"I'll answer my own question, then. You're still holding out the tiniest little hope that this is all a great big misunderstanding."

"I'm doing no such thing. Although..." She wrestled with her doubts.

"Although what?"

She tried to speak carelessly, as if it didn't really matter. "It *could* be a big misunderstanding, I suppose."

"Not if what you told Joan is the truth." He gave her a sheepish look. "Oops."

"I knew it! My mother is a blabbermouth." She glared at him because the guilty party wasn't within reach.

"Mothers are people. They're not perfect." He managed to keep a straight face when he said that. "I imagine it's hard to watch your only child screw up."

"I'm not a mother so I wouldn't know." That was another thing that galled her, and she blamed Jack. Married almost seven years—her heart gave a little leap; seven years on Valentine's Day, the last day of the cruise—and not a child in sight.

At first they'd been too immature to consider having a child, and then they'd been too selfish and caught up in the acquisition of *things*. For the past couple of years she'd begun to suffer from baby hunger, but the right time to start a family had never materialized. Instead, she and Jack had grown apart until now it looked as if she'd probably never know the joys of bearing his child.

"Don't look so sad," Bart said. "You're lucky you don't have children, the way things are."

"You know nothing about 'the way things are,'" she snapped.

"I know about Rusti."

Her heart plummeted, but still she felt compelled to ask, "What about Rusti?"

"He's sleeping with her. What else?"

"You don't know that!" She jumped to her feet, hands clenched at her sides.

He stood up more slowly. "Be reasonable, Ivy. Where else would he be sleeping? You threw him out of your cabin. He had to go somewhere, and it only stands to reason—"

"I'll thank you not to spread rumors like that without proof," she said through stiff lips.

"I stand corrected." He dipped his head in a slight bow. "But you're living in a fantasy world if you think for a minute that—"

"I *think* we'd better say good-night." She stood before him with her shoulders back and her entire body stiff and unforgiving. "Thank you for the wine with dinner, and for the show."

"Stop it," he said irritably. "I don't expect to buy you with a bottle of wine or a show that's free, anyway."

"If you're smart, you don't expect to buy me at all," she said tartly. "I'm not for sale." *But I'm available,* she thought sadly, and here she was spitting in the eye of the most likely man on board this ship.

IVY LAY BACK on a lounge chair in the shadows at the edge of a small cluster of stargazers on the bow of A Deck. It must be after midnight, she thought idly, feeling calmer and more relaxed than she had been since boarding this ship.

She was sorry if she'd offended Bart but glad he'd left her alone at last. She needed space and could think of no more enjoyable way to get it than to become lost in the stars. Staring up at the glittering night sky, she felt a pleasant wave of dizziness wash over her. She almost felt as if she might soar off into the heavens if she didn't hold on to the edges of her lounge chair.

Their guide to the wonders of the universe—a young woman who'd arrived wearing an *Inamorata II* T-shirt and trim navy trousers—spoke soothingly over a speaker system. "Since the beginning of time, men—and women, too, I'm sure—have looked up at the sky in amazement. We marvel at the sun and moon, the fiery tails of meteors and comets. But for many of us, the source of greatest wonder has always been . . . the stars."

Lulled by that hypnotic voice, Ivy stared up into the universe and sighed, letting herself drift and dream of what might have been. Why, oh why, had her life come down to this?

"You don't need binoculars or telescopes to see many of the wonders of the heavens." The mesmerizing voice pulled her back, soothed and distracted her. "With the naked eye you can see more than you ever dreamed . . . if you know where to look and what to look for. . . ."

And sometimes, even if you don't, Ivy thought. For sure she had seen more with her naked eyes than she'd ever dreamed.

"Imagine that this celestial sphere is an enormous hollow ball. Earth is at the center with stars on the inside surface, parading by as the Earth rotates...."

Overcome by the brilliance overhead, feeling the effects of a long and exhausting day, Ivy closed her eyes. That soothing voice droned on, speaking of magical things that danced across her imagination.

Deck chairs squeaked, an occasional awe-filled murmur penetrated her consciousness, but little more, for she was struggling with her own question of cosmic importance. And she knew the decision she made now would determine the course of the rest of her life. Then again, maybe Jack had already done that for her.

Until she evened the score, there wasn't any decision to make, really. And here was Bart, ready-made for the task. Why did she hesitate? And why did she cling to Mitchell Kerr like a security blanket when—

Adrift on a soothing cloud of perfumed night air and soothing patter, a faint jarring of her chaise longue disturbed her reverie. Opening one eye, she saw a dark shadow bending over her....

8

IVY HAD ALWAYS LIKED surprises, especially romantic surprises. And what could be more romantically surprising than a kiss from a mystery man?

And with an unfaithful husband she very much *wanted* to be kissed, so as to assuage severe doubts about her current ability to enchant. Whoever this dark shadow might turn out to be, she intended to make the most of him.

Easy enough to think, since she never doubted for a moment that it was Bart... Or, possibly but not likely, Mitchell; such a move seemed totally out of character for him. Either way, though, whichever one it was would be acceptable to her at the moment.

Whichever, she was in the clear. She hadn't asked for this; she hadn't led anyone on. Strong hands settled on her shoulders and she sighed, trying to convince herself that she'd been lying here half-asleep and defenseless. If some strange man kissed her and she...didn't hate it...and decided to go to bed with him, she wouldn't feel guilty. She hadn't started this, Jack had.

So she kept her eyes closed, let her body go limp and receptive and resorted to telepathy: *Whoever you are, don't screw up now!*

A warm, firm mouth touched the corner of hers... trailed to the opposite corner to place little nibbling kisses there. Warm, firm hands massaged her shoulders before sliding down her arms to the elbows....

Next, he placed a kiss full on her mouth, his tongue nudging her lips apart insistently while one hand moved smoothly to cover her breast—

So much for fantasy. She sat up abruptly.

"Damn it!" She gave him a shove that landed him on his butt with a soft grunt of surprised protest. "I'd know that kiss anywhere, Jack Conrad!" she yelled.

"Shhhh! Shhhh!"

At the chorus of disapproval she lowered her voice. "Of all the low-down, contemptible—"

"Shut up, Ivy," he growled. "If you wanna yell, let's at least find a private place to go at it."

A chubby woman on the nearest lounge glared in their direction. "I should hope so," she said in indignant tones. "My goodness, this isn't the Love Boat, you know! There are families around here, little children who could be corrupted by such goings-on!"

"For Pete's sake, lady, what's wrong with kissing my own wife?"

"Shut up, Jack." Ivy sprang from the chaise, her mellow mood completely shot. Grabbing his arm, she dragged him to his feet and pulled him down the deck away from the affronted stargazers.

Once they were alone, she confronted him. "You've got a nerve!"

"I don't think it takes much nerve to kiss my own wife."

"It does if you have to sneak up on her to do it."

"I didn't sneak. I walked right up. You looked like you were a million miles away. In fact, I thought you were asleep."

"I wasn't."

"Now you tell me." He glared at her. "But you knew it was me. If you didn't want me kissing you, why didn't you speak up sooner?"

"Because I *didn't* know it was you, you jerk, at least at first. I had no idea who it was until—"

"You—you—*you didn't know?* Who the hell did you think it was?"

"None of your business."

"The hell it's not! Are you telling me you were lying there thinking about another man?"

"It'd be pretty dumb of me to be thinking about you, now wouldn't it?" She stalked toward the stairwell leading to the deck below.

He tagged along at her elbow. "You were thinking about Bart Van Horny."

"Cute, Jack. Really, really cute."

He caught her arm and swung her around at the head of the stairs. His eyes blazed into hers; she hadn't seen him this worked up in years. Although when they were courting, he used to come at her like a hungry tiger....

His full mouth tilted up in something less than a smile. "Think I'm funny, do you? I'll show you funny."

Slipping one hand around the back of her neck with a speed that boggled the mind, he dragged her hard against him and kissed her.

And she... She kissed him back, damn it. His tongue probed at her lips, and she offered no resistance. His ardor stunned her; it had been such a long time since she'd felt such burning need in him . . . in herself.

But this was wrong! He had no right to make her feel this way, all weak and wanting. With a superhuman effort, she twisted her head aside. His mouth careened across her cheek and found her ear, which he proceeded to nibble.

"Stop that!" she commanded in a voice that shook.

"Why? I like it. So do you." With every word, his soft breath caressed her ear.

She groaned. "This doesn't change anything."

"Let me come back to our stateroom and convince you otherwise."

He grabbed her bottom with one hand and pulled her hips against him hard. She wiggled—trying to break free, nothing else—and it was his turn to groan.

"Ivy, this is supposed to be our second honeymoon. I love you, baby. I've never said that to another woman, I swear, not even when I was trying to get them into bed."

It took just a second for his words to sink in. "Damn you, Jack!" She shoved him away, surprised she was still capable of standing on her own two feet, let alone nearly knocking him off his.

He blinked, frowned, reached for her again. "What'd I say?"

"I'm supposed to take comfort in the fact that you didn't profess your love for Rusti or Wal-Mart—"

"That's Tiffani!"

"—to get them in bed?"

"That's not what I—" All at once, her meaning seemed to sink in. Looking flustered, he blurted out, "I meant, *before* I met you."

"Sure you did." Turning, she hurtled down the stairs, clinging to the hardwood railing for badly needed balance.

He hurtled right behind her. "It's true! But before I met you, there were other women. Hell, Ivy, you knew that. Just because you lived like a nun doesn't mean that I—"

Stopping short at the first landing, she swung around to confront him. "What gave you the idea I lived like a nun?" she challenged.

"Why, because . . . I just—" He frowned. "When I confessed all my past sins . . . you never said . . . you mean, you *didn't?*"

"I did. I really did," she reassured him in a tone guaranteed to drive him mad. "I just wondered how you knew. I guess you just *assumed.*" She whirled and took off again, walking fast.

"Damn it, Ivy!" He hurried after her, as she'd expected. "Is there something you're not telling me? Because if there is—"

At the door to her cabin, she faced him again, her card key in her hand. "Because if there is, what?" she challenged. "Let's stick to the subject, here. You're the one who betrayed our marriage vows. You're the one who slept with another woman—or maybe we should make that *women.* You're the one—"

"I didn't do any of that stuff, not with Tiffani and not with Rusti. I'd never—"

"Gee, why don't I believe you?" Turning her back on him, she thrust home the card key, stepped inside and slammed the door in his face.

Not too surprisingly, he took out his frustration on that same door, pounding with a frustration that vibrated the entire stateroom. But she didn't let him in.

She didn't dare. If he got one foot inside this cabin, the war between the Conrads would be over. And oh, how she'd hate herself in the morning.

IVY LAY IN THE DARKNESS staring out—maybe glaring out—at the mysterious sea. She had really, truly thought the dark shadow leaning over her on deck was Bart.

Damn it, she'd *wanted* it to be Bart. She'd wanted him to kiss her silly, then carry her off to his cabin and make mad, passionate love to her.

And she'd wanted to enjoy it . . . but not *too* much. Bart was not the kind of man who appealed to her when she was in her right mind. He was too . . . something. Too predatory, she decided. He was the kind of man who was always on the prowl, not the kind who would ever commit to one woman, even if he loved her and she loved him.

He wasn't like Jack. Correction, he wasn't like she'd thought Jack was. Apparently all men were alike, in the final analysis, just as her mother always said. Let some sweet young thing shake her booty, and all bets were off.

Ivy rolled over in bed, turning her back on the vast emptiness of the ocean, but not the vast emptiness in her heart. She told herself that Bart was just the kind of man she now needed to do what had to be done.

Once the chase was over, he'd lose interest. There would be no sticky, emotional scenes, no ties, no feelings of guilt or betrayal.

Not on his part, anyway. Who *knew* how she was going to feel?

ON IVY'S MORNING RUN, Jack fell in beside her with a smile as sunny as the day. Not by word or gesture did he indicate he even remembered what had passed between them the previous night.

That really ruffled her feathers. She tried to ignore him, but it was hard. He looked really good, dressed all in blazing white: white shorts, white T-shirt, white jock shoes. Tall, tanned and terrific, he caused female heads to turn when he passed, and no doubt, female hearts to flutter.

Including Rusti's. When they jogged past the tall redheaded dancer, she gave them a friendly wave before turning back to a pudgy passenger trying to coordinate arms and legs in the classic jumping jack.

At the conclusion of her laps, Ivy peeled off in favor of the shade of a canopy. Grabbing a snowy towel from a stack nearby, she patted her damp face, pushing tendrils of hair back behind her terry cloth headband.

Jack was suddenly beside her. "Nice workout," he said, taking up a towel of his own. "Have you had breakfast?"

She gave him a narrow glance. "I had coffee in my room."

"That's not nearly enough for a growing girl," he said with a charming smile. "Let me bring you something." He indicated the poolside buffet.

She edged away. "I don't think that's a good idea."

"It's a great idea," he insisted. "Let me bring you a plate of fruit. Find a nice spot over there in the shade by the rail and I'll surprise you."

She sighed. He knew her weaknesses, all right. She tried to be strong. "I don't know, Jack...."

But he smiled and turned toward the buffet line. Knowing she shouldn't, she made her way to the rail and found a table protected from the light breeze by a Plexiglas panel. She hadn't slept very well last night and had hoped a hard run this morning would work off some of the tension she was feeling.

She wouldn't call it *sexual* tension, exactly. But if that's what it was, even a little bit, she was determined that Jack wouldn't tie her up in those kinds of knots again, thank you very much.

He returned bearing a tray loaded with all sorts of delicacies, things he knew she loved—fresh fruit salad, a tall glass of iced raspberry tea, croissants and tiny flaky pastries. "Where's yours?" she asked. He wasn't all that big on fruit and fancy nibbles. He was more a steak-and-potatoes, beer-and-hotdogs kind of guy.

"I thought we could share," he said, pulling out a chair and sitting down.

"But you don't like this stuff," she objected, reaching for a big, ripe strawberry.

"I like sharing," he said in a husky voice that froze her hand in midair.

Even with her mouth half-open to receive the berry, she redirected the juicy red fruit from her mouth to his. Damn, it was almost like being hypnotized. He parted his lips and she slipped the berry inside, past his straight white teeth.

Somehow she found her gaze locked with his. Before she could withdraw her hand, he'd closed his lips around her fingertips. When he sucked gently, she gasped; she couldn't help it. Her heart thundered in her ears. Aware that *he* was aware of her every nuance, she still couldn't control her physical reactions.

She snatched her hand away. Without thinking, she pressed her fingers against her own mouth, tasting the flavor of strawberry, where his tongue had touched her skin.

"Oh, my," she murmured, unable to tear her gaze from his. "Oh, my goodness—"

At that precise moment, a new voice intruded upon the intimacy of the moment. "Here you are, Ivy. I meant to catch up with you after our morning run, but I got sidetracked by a tour lecture."

It was Bart. Close behind him was Mitchell, who did not look pleased to be there.

Much to her surprise, Jack seemed indifferent to the interruption. She wondered indignantly if he'd failed to feel the same jolting connection that had just rocked her.

Listening to the three men exchange small talk, she brooded. Maybe that's why Jack had been unfaithful. Maybe he no longer felt that spark, that fire that had blazed between them during the early days of their relationship.

Worse, the possibility existed that he might be right. If she could find that same connection with another man, as he had apparently found it with other women, that would pretty much prove that what she once had with Jack hadn't been real in the first place.

Such thoughts depressed her, even in these glamorous surroundings. When Mitchell brought up the masked Valentine costume ball, she was more than ready to be diverted.

"It sounds like fun," she agreed, "but I didn't bring a costume." She darted an accusing glance at Jack. "I got distracted and forgot."

"Not to worry," Mitchell reassured her. "The ship provides a variety of disguises for the unprepared. In fact, I've always chosen my costume here. Would you like me to show you the wardrobe department?"

"Why not?" She stood up, ready to put some distance between herself and her husband. When he was surly and unreasonable, she had trouble resisting him. When he was being charming...

Mitchell, not privy to her thoughts, said to Jack, "Would you care to join us?"

"Ummm..." Jack hesitated. "Think I'll pass. Maybe I'll see you at one of the shows tonight."

"I wouldn't doubt it," Mitchell agreed. "Are you ready, Ivy?"

"Hey," Bart said. "I'll go along. Last time I cruised this ship, I didn't go to the masquerade ball and regretted it when everybody told me what a great time they'd had."

Mitchell did not look pleased. "Very well. It's this way."

Ivy took a step, then couldn't resist one final glance back at Jack. "Aren't you going to the masked ball?"

"I haven't made up my mind yet." He smiled, that slow unfolding smile that had always sent little tremors of excitement skittering through her. "Would you like me to?"

"I'd like you to do whatever you'd like to do," she said, but couldn't manage the airy indifference she'd hoped to achieve.

"And I'd like to do what you'd like me to do whether I like it or—"

"Children, children! Not again!" Smiling, Mitchell led her away.

"WELL, WELL, WELL," the pudgy little wardrobe mistress said, eyeing Ivy. "What do I still have that will fit this absolutely stunning creature?"

Ivy laughed, not taking the comment seriously for a second. "I'll bet you say that to all your cruisers."

"Believe me," the woman said fervently, "I don't!" She walked in a circle around Ivy. Mitchell and Bart moved out of her way. Inspection completed, she planted her hands on her ample hips. "Okay, here's the deal. I've got two costumes that should do for you."

Ivy cocked her head. "And they are?"

"Scheherazade and Little Mary Sunshine."

"Scheherazade?"

"You know, the harem girl who told great stories to keep some king from separating her head from her body." The wardrobe mistress gestured at her own throat and made graphic slicing sounds.

Mitchell cleared his throat. "That's close," he conceded. "She was the wife of a sultan of India."

The little woman shrugged. "Same difference," she said agreeably.

Bart guffawed. "And the other choice is Little Mary Who?"

"Sunshine. It's a blue gingham dress, a white apron and sunbonnet, Mary Janes—that kind of thing. It's so sweet it tends to give people sugar attacks."

"I'm hardly the sweet type," Ivy confessed.

"I don't know about that," Bart interjected. "I think you're very sweet."

"Actually," the wardrobe mistress said, "I see you more as the Scheherazade type."

"Now that," Ivy said, "is even more of a stretch." She reached up to ruffle the blond fringe of her shaggy haircut.

"Not to worry," the woman said airily. "The costume comes with a black wig and enough veils to confuse the issue."

"Sheer veils, naturally," Ivy guessed.

"There is a reason the costume's still available," the woman agreed with a smile. "Here, let me get it so you can take a look."

She returned minutes later carrying a large wardrobe box, which she proceeded to open. Through layers of tissue paper, a costume emerged—a very scanty costume made up mostly of beads and "jewels" and many yards of sheer fabric in pastel shades of pink and blue and lavender.

Ivy had to laugh. "I don't think so," she said. "Can I take a look at Little Mary's outfit?"

"Okay, but it does seem a shame. I think you could do this one justice, which is more than I can say for the last woman who wore it." Looking disappointed, she put the box aside.

"There's method to her madness," Bart put in, indicating Ivy. "She has a jealous husband and he wouldn't like it if she showed up wearing something like this." He reached into the box, picking up a filmy handful.

That remark ruffled Ivy's feathers. "That has nothing to do with it at all," she declared.

"In that case, I apologize," Bart said, not looking in the least repentant. "But you've got to admit, if you arrived dressed in seven veils and little else, you'd get to good old Jack big-time. That's all I meant to say."

Mitchell looked disapproving. "If Ivy's not comfortable wearing such a skimpy costume—"

"It isn't that," Ivy said. "I've worn bikinis. This wouldn't be so bad—in a swimming pool, anyway. But in a ballroom..."

The wardrobe mistress looked hopeful. "You'd be the belle of the ball, that's for sure. But if you want to go as Little Mary, far be it from me—"

"I don't," Ivy decided, giving in to her worst instincts. It *would* get to Jack. Besides, she'd be wearing a mask and nobody would know it was her. Except Mitchell, Bart, and of course, Jack, who knew her body, just as she knew his kiss.

Or, he had, once upon a time.

9

"RUSTI, I'VE GOT A PROBLEM," Jack understated.

Rusti looked up from the sheet music she'd been perusing. Rehearsal had just ended and she was the last to leave the stage.

She gave him a brilliant if somewhat absent smile. "What is it, Jackie? You look worried."

"You could say that."

She leapt lightly off the stage. He fell in beside her, and together they walked to the nearest table and sat down, all alone in the cavernous show room.

She patted his cheek with a manicured hand. "Tell Rusti everything."

"The ship docks in Martinique tomorrow, right?"

"Right. That's a problem?"

"It's part of the problem. Thanks to you, the crew's been putting me up in the last vacant bunk in their quarters. Now Desmond tells me we're picking up another waiter when we dock tomorrow. That means I'll have to give up my bed—or rather, his bed."

"You poor little thing." She shook her head in sympathy. "I swear, this is the fullest cruise I've ever been on. There's not an inch of extra space anywhere. Except..." She narrowed her green eyes thoughtfully.

"Except where?" Agitated, Jack shoved his hair away from his forehead. "Damn, I'll take anything. I'd sleep under a table if they'd let me, but I've already tried that route and it didn't work out."

"It's frowned on," she agreed with a smile.

"So what's your idea? I've even considered the lifeboats. If worse came to worst, maybe I could—"

She let out a little yelp of alarm. "The captain would kill you if you got caught, and then he'd kill every member of the crew who ever spoke to you. That covers most of us, at this point."

"I was afraid of that."

She patted his hand. "You look like somebody's been kickin' your dog. Hon, if nothin' else opens up, you can always stay with me."

"Yeah, you and your roommate. Talk about a happy trio."

She laughed. "As a matter of fact...my roommate has moved in with one of the ship's officers."

Jack was astonished. "She can do that?"

"She can if she's invited. Hey, happens all the time. I'd have mentioned this before, but I thought you were all set. That and..."

He gave her a suspicious look. "And what?"

"I didn't think your wife would much like the idea of you bunkin' with me," she said frankly. "Can't say I'd blame her, either."

"She's got no room to complain," he declared righteously, even knowing Rusti was absolutely correct. A little shiver of pure terror rippled down his spine. Ivy was already suspicious. If she found out for sure that he was sharing a room with Rusti, there'd be hell to pay.

Rusti looked sympathetic. "She's your wife, sugar. I know she's mad at you, but she'll get over it if you just keep your cool. That's why I didn't say anything before now." She stood up on those long, lovely legs. "But you may have no choice. I lucked out this cruise, got into the high-rent district. I've got twin beds in my stateroom, which is on B Deck. If worse comes to worst..." She shrugged.

"Thanks, Rusti," he said. "You're a real pal."

She winked and blew him a kiss. "Would Ivy see it that way?"

IVY INTENDED TO GO ASHORE at Martinique. Mitchell had gallantly offered to show her around the French-flavored tropical paradise, which he'd visited many times with his wife. Unfortunately, just as they were preparing to join cruisers streaming down the gang-plank, she saw Jack join the line ahead of her. Immediately she got cold feet.

"You go ahead," she told Mitchell. "The last thing I want to do is spend the day avoiding Jack."

Mitchell looked at her long and hard. "Are you sure that's what you really mean?" he asked at last.

Ivy frowned. "Of course. What else?"

He shrugged. "Only you know the answer to that, Ivy." He moved on. "I'll see you at dinner, then."

"Yes, at dinner."

Feeling somehow bereft, she watched him join the stream of disembarking cruisers. Seeing Jack had thrown her, and now she was sorry she'd taken the coward's way out. What was she going to do with herself for the rest of the day, practically alone on this great big boat?

IVY SAT in the darkened movie theater aboard the *Inamorata II,* having a hard time believing she'd stooped to watching some inane spy flick, when she could have been living it up on a tropical island, or even elsewhere on this ship. By rights, she should be lying on some beach, or at the very least, beside the pool on A Deck. There was absolutely no excuse for sitting alone, brooding in the dark.

Someone slipped into the seat beside hers. She stiffened and leaned away, annoyed that in a nearly empty room some stranger would presume so. Only when the scene on the movie screen shifted to a bright outdoor shot did a surreptitious glance tell her it wasn't a stranger at all who had invaded her space.

Bart murmured, "Good flick?"

"No."

"Why don't we get out of here, then?"

She hesitated only briefly. "Why not?"

On A Deck, he found a secluded table with a view of the bustling port city of Fort-de-France. Hailing a passing waiter, he ordered them both the cocktail of the day: a Miami Whammy. The waiter said: "Rum and orange and pineapple and lotsa good stuff. You'll like it, m'lady."

She did, too. Sipping, she sighed and leaned back in her chair, closing her eyes against the glare of a bright Caribbean sun. It had rained earlier in the day—as it did every day in these parts, which accounted for the humidity, she supposed.

"I thought you were going ashore," she said idly to Bart.

"I thought *you* were going ashore," he countered.

"Changed my mind at the last minute."

"That's about the time I changed mine."

"What a coincidence." She gave him a lazy, indifferent smile.

He shrugged. "There's a wine and cheese tasting tonight. Do you plan to go?"

"I haven't made up my mind."

He regarded her with narrowed eyes. "It seems to me you're having a hell of a difficult time making up your mind about anything these days."

She shifted in her chair, placing her drink glass on the table. "Maybe," she admitted irritably. "But at the risk of sounding rude, I must point out that it's really no concern of yours."

He smiled, obviously having taken no offense. "But what will I tell your mother when she asks if her only child had a good time?"

"Tell her—! No, don't tell her that, she'd wash my mouth out with soap. Tell her you have no idea, which will be the truth." Ivy stood up. "I'm feeling restless. I think I'll stroll around the deck for a while."

"I'll stroll with you." He rose just as promptly.

"Bart—"

"Ivy—"

Their glances locked, hers annoyed, his intense. Without warning, he stepped forward, put his arms around her and kissed her. Shocked to the soles of her feet, she stood like a stick of wood and let him have his way with her mouth.

But all the time she was wondering what in the world she had found so appealing about this man. What did he have in Florida that he didn't have now?

What did *she* have then that she didn't have now, besides Jack?

Bart stepped away, and she saw a faint flush color his cheekbones; a puzzled expression entered his eyes. "If I didn't know better," he said, "I'd think you were a real iceberg."

"Whether I am or not, you shouldn't have done that."

"I shouldn't have done it in Florida, either, but I did. And you liked it at the time."

Now it was *her* cheeks that grew warm. "Let's don't talk about Florida," she said. "Florida was... temporary insanity." In more ways than one.

"Not necessarily." He seemed to regain composure at the same rate she lost it. "This is the nineties, Ivy. Divorce doesn't carry the stigma it once did."

"Divorce!" She stared at him, aghast. "Now you *are* presuming too much."

"Maybe, but I've come too far to stop now. What happened between you and Jack?"

"None of your business."

"He was unfaithful, am I right? He slept with another woman and you found out."

"I thought my mother the blabbermouth told you all about it."

"Let's just say she hinted."

"Gosh, Bart, that's the first time I ever knew you to *take* a hint," she drawled, good and mad now. "If you'll excuse me, I think I'll take a nap before dinner."

He didn't bat an eye at her dismissive tone. "Do that, Ivy. And while you're at it, try to figure out what it is you want... before it's too late."

Great. Just what she needed. The voice of doom echoing in her head all the way to her cabin.

He was right, though. She should just go to bed with him and get it over with.

Maybe she still would. . . .

A SOFT RAPPING announced the arrival of the salad and iced tea she'd ordered from room service. She opened the door to a smiling Desmond.

"I have good things for you, m'lady," he promised, walking inside to set his tray on a small table. "A fruit salad, very fresh—" He lifted a large crystal bowl from the tray. "A pitcher of raspberry tea, also very fresh." That joined the salad, as did two tall glasses already filled with ice.

"It looks wonderful," she agreed, "but why did you bring two glasses?"

Her question appeared to puzzle him. "Your mister's with you now, right?" He rolled his eyes. "Ah, m'lady, if you knew how he suffered!"

She had to laugh at his theatrics. "You've watched him do it, I suppose," she teased, but there was an edge to the remark. Picking up a plump grape, she popped it into her mouth.

Desmond nodded vigorously. "All the time," he vowed. Taking a single long-stemmed red rose from the tray, he presented it to her with a flourish. "He says, give you flowers on every tray, only you don't ask for much."

More than you realize, she thought. "If you see him around, tell him I said he's wasting his time and probably his money." Nevertheless, she accepted the rose and automatically raised it to her nose.

"I been seein' him, all right, every night." Desmond poured tea. "I don't think he be likin' that."

Ivy, thoroughly confused, accepted the glass. "Every night?"

Desmond nodded. "Sure. He been sleepin' in that extra bunk, only now—"

Ivy's head snapped up and she interrupted sharply. "What extra bunk?"

Desmond's dark eyes widened. "In th' crew quarters, m'lady. Where else you think that man been sleepin', after you throwed him outa his own bed?"

Ivy laughed out loud. "I thought maybe he'd found a nice table or something to crawl under."

"He tried that, but it didn't work." Desmond answered her frivolous remark seriously. "Then his frien' Rusti, she ask us to put the poor mon up. Ever'body likes that Rusti so no problem! But now ever'body likes that Jack, too, and we hopin' you'll take the poor mon back now that he—"

Ivy's laughter interrupted the flow of words. She felt almost light-headed with relief at these revelations. "Desmond," she said, "you're a treasure!"

The look he gave her plainly said *he* thought *she* was some kind of a nut.

After he'd gone, Ivy stood there for a long time with her hands clasped at her waist, mulling it all over.

So Jack *wasn't* sharing close quarters with Rusti Wheeler. Talk about relieved!

On the other hand, it was too soon to break out the champagne for a reconciliation, even to please her cabin steward.

She and Jack still had Dallas to deal with.

JACK WAS DISGUSTED, just plain disgusted. He'd gone ashore hoping—hell, expecting—to hook up with Ivy and Mitchell. He'd eventually found Mitchell, but Ivy hadn't been with him.

So Jack had sulked through the French-flavored streets of Fort-de-France, having a thoroughly miserable time. He felt even worse when it finally dawned on him that he hadn't seen Bart Van Horn, either. If his *wife* had stayed on the ship for a tryst with that Florida land raper...!

Jack boarded the *Inamorata II* in a foul mood. The first person he saw was Mitchell Kerr, who took one look at the scowling countenance before him and mentioned a drink.

Jack accepted, wondering what Mitchell was looking so grim about. Over a beer he tried to decide where the older man fit into all this.

To break the silence, Jack said, "I saw you ashore earlier. I thought Ivy would be with you, but I guess she changed her mind."

"That's right." Mitchell sipped his Scotch and soda. "Frankly, I don't think she wanted to run into you."

"I figured." Jack glared into his glass of beer. "I suppose she stayed behind with old Van Horny."

"I don't believe Mr. Van Horn had anything to do with her decision. In fact, I'd bet on that."

"I'm glad to hear it." Distinctly uncomfortable, Jack looked around the lounge, everywhere except at the older man. "Uhhh...has Ivy told you...I mean, has she confided in you about—"

The ensuing silence was the longest Jack could recall. At last Mitchell let him off the hook. "You mean, about what happened in Dallas?"

"Jeez, then she has."

"I believe she felt the need to talk to someone and considered me to be a safe choice."

"*Are* you a safe choice?"

"I like to think so. My only concern is her well-being, if that's what you mean."

"Me, too." Jack drained his glass and signaled a waiter. "Mitch, old buddy, I didn't do it. I'm innocent."

"Are you?"

A question, but curiously nonjudgmental. Jack nodded vigorously. "As a newborn lamb—well, almost that innocent." And he did feel sheepish saying it. "I've got a buddy back home who said I must have known what Tiffani—that's the woman's name, Tiffani—was up to."

"You're a pilot, I understand. The woman involved is a stewardess?"

"Jeez, don't call her that! She's a flight attendant—gotta be politically correct and all."

"That's not what Ivy calls her."

"Yeah, Ivy calls her *Wal*-Mart!"

Mitchell stifled a smile. "Among other things."

"Mitch, old buddy, when I stopped to think about it, I had to admit to myself that I knew Tiff was trying to hit on me. I've also got to admit, I was a little flattered. She's a cute kid—nothing special, not like Ivy, but a cute kid. And what could happen with a whole bunch of us at that bar?"

"But something happened somewhere."

"Yeah, later. She followed me home." Jack raised his right hand as a pledge. "I swear to God, I didn't invite her. She said I'd forgotten to pick up my change and she was just being nice returning it."

"That's when your wife walked in?"

"Well...not exactly." Jack, although completely innocent of any *real* wrongdoing, couldn't help squirming a bit. "Tiff...ah...she sort of *kissed* me."

"She kissed you and that's when Ivy walked in?"

"Not exactly." Jack grabbed a respite by offering plastic and signing for his beer, but he was only delaying the inevitable.

Mitchell gave his companion an enigmatic look. "You don't have to explain any of this to me, you know."

"I want to," Jack insisted staunchly. "You seem to be the best friend she's got on this boat. It's important to me that you understand I'm...I'm not *all* bad."

"Jack, I never presumed to judge."

"Then just listen, okay? Tiffani kissed me and I guess I kissed her back—hell, I know I kissed her back. But that's *all* I did, because I knew that if our positions were reversed, Ivy wouldn't let some guy come on to her. Ivy's a great girl, true-blue and all that. She'd never even look at another guy and there I was—" He choked off the words, swallowing hard, wondering how he could have been so stupid.

"Sounds to me like a bad case of seven-year itch," Mitchell said.

"It's an itch, all right, but—" Jack stopped short. "You mean, like in that Marilyn Monroe movie? Trust me, Tiff's no Marilyn."

"And apparently you, my boy, are no Tom Ewell." A smile twitched around Mitchell's mouth. "That is, unless you've been secretly fantasizing about your little airport groupy."

"I've been fantasizing, all right," Jack said grimly, "but it's been about my wife." *My wife and another man,* he added silently. "I've got to find a way to make this up to her before . . . well, before . . ."

"Before she makes good her threat and sleeps with another man. Say it, Jack. Face it—because she may very well *do* it if you don't figure out some way to convince her of your sterling qualities."

"I know what she threatened . . . but I don't think she really would . . ." Jack stumbled around for words he almost, but not quite, believed.

Mitchell shrugged. "I'm not sure, to tell you the truth. I've only known the lady for a couple of days. Unfortunately, the situation is complicated by the ever-present Bart Van Horn, who stands ready to volunteer for any period of duty she'd care to allot him."

"I'll kill him," Jack vowed in a choked voice. "I swear, I'll kill that son of a—!"

"Unless he worms his way considerably further into her affections, you'll have no need," Mitchell said quickly. "But if you wait until the need is there, it'll be too late."

"Go to hell," Jack said roughly.

"Don't shoot the messenger, pal."

"Who should I shoot, then?"

"Perhaps yourself. At the risk of seeming indelicate, are you sleeping with your friend, Miss Wheeler?"

Jack choked on his beer. "Am I what? You think I—of all the—"

"Spare me your righteous indignation," Mitchell suggested mildly. "It has been suggested by others— not me—that such is the case."

"It sure as hell is not the case!" Finally Jack had found a reason to be indignant. "I've been sleeping in an extra bunk in the crew's quarters. They took me in when no one else, including my own wife, would."

"Good," Mitchell said, "because if you were sharing quarters with the delectable Ms. Wheeler, and Ivy found out about it, I suspect it would be the final straw."

"Rusti's just an old school buddy, like I said."

Mitchell looked close to smiling. "I'm pleased to hear it." He glanced at his wristwatch and stood. "I've got to dress for dinner. I'm delighted we had this little talk. I really would like to see you two kids get back together."

"Thanks." Jack's grin felt more sincere. "I need all the friends I can get."

Mitchell, in the process of turning away, stopped short. "Please don't misunderstand," he said. "I'd like to see the two of you together, but Ivy is my first concern. Not you. Ivy."

Jack nodded.

"I'm quite fond of her," Mitchell went on. "In some ways she..." He smiled suddenly. "She reminds me of my wife. If I can help her...protect her, I'll do it. Even if it's not in your best interests."

Jack didn't know what he was supposed to say about that, so he just shrugged and let it go. But when he was alone, he thought about it...and wondered just how much like Mitchell's wife Ivy might be.

10

THAT EVENING at the wine and cheese tasting, Ivy watched Jack with a new awareness. Now that she knew there was nothing between him and Rusti, she felt more disposed to give him the benefit of other doubts as well.

The big jerk couldn't help it if he was incredibly appealing to women, she supposed. She watched him fetch a napkin for a large lady in blue crepe, a plate of cheese cubes for a giggly and gawky twenty-something female. Both looked at him with adoring eyes.

Jack was nice to all women. As a matter of fact, he was nice to everyone.

Until he had a reason not to be, she amended, watching her husband's glance zero in on Bart Van Horn, then narrow almost imperceptibly in a silent challenge.

"More wine?" Bart asked.

"More cheese?" Mitchell chimed in.

Suddenly she felt hemmed in, smothered. How was she going to find an appropriate sinner in this mob with her unwilling gaze constantly drawn to her husband, and with bodyguards hovering around her at all times?

Watching Jack move toward them through the throng, so tall and lean in the tuxedo he'd bought just for this cruise, she felt herself weakening. He was the best-looking man on this ship, and the most charming, and the most appealing.

She realized that she was actually hovering on the verge of...of...forgiving him! She had to stem the flow of her thoughts.

She had to stand firm. That's why, when he made his way to her side and asked what she was doing later, she practically jumped down his throat, ending with, "And you'd better stop following me around! I don't have to account for my whereabouts to you, Jack Conrad!" Then she stormed away.

JACK TOOK HER abrupt departure philosophically, although he was keenly disappointed. Tonight would have been the perfect time for them to get back together. If she'd given up her stupid game and forgiven him, that would have canceled out his other "problem."

She hadn't, though, so he still had to find a place to bunk down for the night. Changing into jeans and T-shirt later in Rusti's stateroom, he wedged his tuxedo in with the things he'd stowed there earlier in the day. Rusti had offered to hang on to his stuff until he could find a place to hang his hat—literally. He looked longingly at her extra bed, sighed, opened the door and slipped out.

He had no intention of taking her up on her offer to sleep in her cabin...if he could possibly help it. Surely, somewhere on this tub, he could find a place to sleep that wouldn't put him any deeper into his wife's portable doghouse.

AT TWO the following morning, Jack found himself standing bleary-eyed in the corridor outside Rusti's door, knocking with soft insistence. Her stateroom was on the same deck as the casino, which meant some traffic even at this hour.

Hearing laughter, he glanced around uneasily. There was a knot of people passing by the end of the hallway. To his relief, he didn't see anyone he knew; all he needed was to be spotted banging on a woman's door at this hour.

"Rusti," he called, increasing the force of his blows slightly but trying to avoid disturbing the peace. "It's me, Jack! Let me in!"

Eventually she did, yawning mightily before stepping aside for his entry. She wore some little ol' wispy pink thing that didn't leave a whole lot to the imagination.

He burst inside and slammed the door closed. "Hallelujah!" he muttered, dropping wearily onto the neat bed, as opposed to the rumpled one from which she'd just arisen. "Nobody knows the troubles I seen."

She pushed a tangle of flaming hair away from her face. "Jack, what the—?" Another yawn before she could finish, then, "What are you doing here? I thought—?"

"Rusti, this has got to be the last empty bed on the entire boat."

"Uh-oh."

"Yeah. I've been all over this tub. I've tried everything, even sleeping under a table in the Lovebird Lounge."

"What happened?"

"They caught me."

"Oh, dear."

He nodded. "At first they thought I was a stowaway. When we finally got that cleared up, they gave me one last drink, which turned out to be a damn good thing, and sent me on my way."

She was having a tough time waking up. He'd seen her dance, the energy she expended, and he understood. "A good thing?"

"Because next I tried to crawl into a lifeboat. One of the officers caught me and we had to go through the whole thing all over again. Only this time I think I got off by convincing him I was drunk instead of just stupid."

She was finally coming awake. "You were lucky, Jackie," she declared. "You could get in a lot of trouble messing with the lifeboats."

"Don't I know it. I feel like I just dodged a bullet." He glanced around her stateroom with a kind of helpless defeat. "They're on the lookout for me now. I couldn't even sneak into a broom closet without getting nailed—which I tried, and I was." He flopped back onto the bed, legs bending at the knee to keep his feet on the floor.

Hell, he felt as if he was acting in some old television sitcom, keeping one foot on the floor at all times to prove nothing was really going on. He stared up at the ceiling. "I'm sorry," he mumbled. "I didn't mean to get you involved in my troubles."

"Hey, no problem. Or rather, the problem will be all yours, if word gets back to you-know-who."

He knew who, all right. He remained motionless while Rusti turned off the lights and crawled back into bed. Tired as he was, he didn't even get undressed. He simply lay there uncomfortably until exhaustion overcame all else and he drifted off to sleep, still hoping that no one had seen him come in here. When the time was right, he didn't want *anything* getting into the way of a reconciliation with Ivy.

WHEN IVY OPENED her eyes shortly after eight the following morning, the ship had already docked in Barbados. She sprang from her bed with new optimism.

Today would not be spent moping around the ship while everyone else went ashore to have a good time, she vowed. Dressing quickly in khaki slacks and a cheerful yellow T-shirt, she bounded downstairs to the dining room.

Only two of her three cavaliers awaited her. Naturally, the missing link was Jack, the one she was most eager to see. Keeping a determined smile on her face, she took her seat and proceeded to eat a hearty breakfast.

"So," Mitchell said at the meal's conclusion, "what are your plans for the day, Ivy?" He dropped his linen napkin beside his plate.

She smiled. "I thought perhaps you'd let me make up for being such a wet blanket yesterday. Are you going ashore?"

He nodded. "There's a beach here that my wife and I always enjoyed," he said softly. "We'd have one of the hotels pack us a lunch and we'd spend the day just soaking up the sun, swimming, exploring...." He sighed. "It may be a mistake, but I thought I'd like to relive those good times."

"Could you use a little company?" Ivy asked. "I'd love to join you. But if you'd prefer to be alone, I'd understand."

"I welcome the company. The ship doesn't leave until six, so we'll have plenty of time." He smiled at her. "But we don't have to spend the entire day at the beach. If you'd rather shop, or take a tour, there are many points of interest in and about Bridgetown."

She shook her head. "A quiet, peaceful day on the beach is just what I need." Would she ever get that infernal *thinking* over with? Every time she neared a decision, something came along and changed her mind.

Bart, who'd been listening with interest, leaned forward. "How about making it a threesome? I wouldn't mind a little fun in the sun myself."

Mitchell's expression grew stern. "Some other time," he said. "I think the lady is looking for something that could easily get lost in a crowd."

Bart frowned. "Ivy?"

"Sorry, Bart," she replied. "I'm afraid this is a private party."

And then a blinding thought struck her; if she still intended to commit adultery, this might be the perfect opportunity. Alone on a tropical beach with an attractive man...

Bart took his dismissal with good grace. "In that case, I think I may just grab a few winks. I closed down the casino last night and didn't get to bed until way past midnight."

Ivy, who had zero interest in gambling, inquired, "Did you win or lose?"

Bart smiled. "The jury's still out on that," he said enigmatically. "Ask me later."

MITCHELL ORDERED their lunch from a hotel constructed, he explained, of the island's golden coral stone. He and Ivy wandered across marble floors beneath slow-moving ceiling fans, through public rooms filled with antiques and flowers and crystal chandeliers. Past open doors, she saw lily ponds, beds of ferns and flowering shrubs. Over all lay a kind of island magic.

"This is exquisite," she said. "Such understated elegance on a tropical island! I never imagined it quite like this."

Mitchell looked pleased. "Barbados offers a real contrast—British reserve on one hand and a kind of island sensuality on the other. Great Britain ruled here for nearly three hundred and fifty years, and it shows. Propriety is still highly valued."

A representative of the hotel, calling Mitchell by name, presented them with a huge wicker picnic basket. Amid much bowing and smiling and good wishes for a successful outing, he snapped his fingers, and their driver and guide for the day appeared to escort them to their car, a thirty-year-old Rolls-Royce.

The drive to the beach wasn't nearly long enough for Ivy, who enjoyed the luxury of the classic vehicle traveling on the left-hand side of the road in the British style. Or at least, that's what she thought until she saw their destination.

A tangle of luxurious vegetation protected the beach itself from prying eyes. Walking beneath coconut palms and shaggy ficus trees, with birds and an occasional bee humming through the steamy air, they quickly broke through the trees onto the beach itself. Ivy caught her breath in appreciation. She'd never seen sand so white and so fine, water or sky so clear and clean a blue.

If only Jack—

She whirled toward Mitchell. "The water looks wonderful. Shall we take a dip before we eat?" She'd put on her swimsuit before they'd left the ship and now she reached for the buttons on her wraparound skirt. "Race you!"

But even while she scrambled, laughing, through the clear water, she couldn't keep her true thoughts from surfacing: *If only Jack were here!*

But it wasn't Jack, it was Mitchell who frolicked beside her. So forget Jack, she ordered herself. In the looks department, Mitchell took a back seat to no man. His body, revealed by a conservative pair of navy blue swim trunks, was as muscular and fit as that of a man half his age.

Impulsively she asked the question on her mind. "Uhh... How old are you, Mitchell?"

"Fifty-five," he said without the slightest hesitation. It was as if he'd been looking for an opportunity to tell her... and perhaps, discourage her.

Boy, was he wrong about that! Mitchell Kerr was a hunk in any age group, and that was a fact. A hunk with plenty of experience in pleasing a woman, she never doubted....

She might as well admit that; the time to put up or shut up was drawing near.

THE CONTENTS of the lunch basket, laid out on a blanket unfolded by their driver, revealed several surprises.

"Try some *buljol*," Mitchell suggested, lifting a forkful. "It's very popular locally."

She took a tentative taste of the unfamiliar concoction. "Fish and...?"

"Codfish marinated with tomatoes and onions and sweet peppers, that sort of thing. We also have sandwiches, if you prefer."

Reaching for a thermos, he poured cups of proper British tea and laid out a packet of proper English biscuits. Dessert was papaya, so sweet and exotic that Ivy groaned with pleasure, and bananas stuffed with a mixture of rum and cashews.

Together they made short work of their lunch.

"That was wonderful," she said when she'd finished. She patted her midriff, beneath the bright red tank suit. "Now that we've eaten, I guess it's all right to ask. Was that codfish raw or was I imagining things?"

"Raw." He gave her a cautious smile. "Does that bother you?"

She shook her head. "Not after the fact, although it shouldn't, anyway. I've had raw fish in a Japanese restaurant before. Jack, on the other hand, won't touch anything that isn't—" She stopped short.

"Don't be reluctant to bring up his name, Ivy." Mitchell refilled his teacup and hers. "He's your husband, after all."

"I know, but—" Chewing on her lower lip, she looked out over the tranquil scene before her. Barbados was everybody's dream of a tropical island come true, made for love and romance. And here she sat, stewing over *him*.

How did you go about propositioning a man who insisted on discussing your husband?

Mitchell sipped his tea. "Don't you think it's time you sat down with Jack and talked this out, Ivy?"

"We *have* talked. It got us nowhere."

"Did you talk or did you fight?"

"What difference does it make? We can't find any common ground. Every time I start thinking we've got a chance, I remember one irrefutable fact—he betrayed me."

"Now you're thinking about betraying *him*. Two wrongs don't make a right."

"Maybe not, but two wrongs will make us even." She shot him a troubled glance. "I'm not going to end up like my mother, Mitchell."

"Your mother?"

"My mother's been married five times. My father was her first husband, and he died when I was twelve." Even now, she ached, remembering that awful time. "In his will, he left a considerable amount of money to a woman I'd never heard of. When I asked my mother about it, she broke down and admitted that he'd been 'carrying on,' as she put it, with that woman for years."

"Poor little Ivy."

"Poor Mother. She'd known all along and looked the other way, afraid of losing him." Ivy squared her shoulders. "I'll never be that needy, Mitchell. I'd rather die than go through the humiliation my mother endured." She gave a bitter little laugh. "Of course, she's made up for it. She's been married and divorced every few years like clockwork ever since Daddy died, and she's taken every one of them to the cleaners. Still..."

Her throat clenched and she couldn't go on.

He patted her hand as if he understood. "You've come this far," he said gently. "Get it all out and perhaps you'll feel better."

"I couldn't feel worse." Her voice was scratchy and she cleared her aching throat. "I thought I was different. I thought Jack was different. When mother teased me about the seven-year itch, I felt so superior. And look what happened!"

Mitchell stood up and she found herself looking at his strong, brown legs. "You don't know what happened," he said, "not really. You know what you saw, but there's at least a slight chance you put the wrong interpretation on it."

"God, I wish! But—" Looking up through a film of tears, she saw—

Impossible. She blinked fast and looked again. This time there could be no doubt; Jack had emerged from the fringe of palms and was walking across the beach toward them.

She gave a little yelp of alarm. "Mitchell! What have you done?"

He sighed. "Given you a chance to save your marriage, I hope." He touched his lips lightly with his fingertips, blowing her a kiss. "Talk to him, Ivy. And perhaps even more important, listen to him... with your heart, this time. I'll be nearby, if you need me."

"Don't go! I'm not sure—"

"Nobody ever is." With a wave of the hand, he trudged away.

"THIS IS a dirty trick, Jack." She lifted her chin and glared up at the man standing before her, tall and gorgeous in shorts and T-shirt. "And here I've been thinking Mitchell was my friend."

Jack bent his long legs and knelt, resting his hands on his thighs. "He is."

"Yeah, right."

"You're hard on your friends, Ivy."

"I certainly am not!"

"No?" He cocked his head, a slight smile touching his wide, mobile mouth. "Take Cathy and Rob, for instance."

"What are you talking about?"

"Rob was just trying to help when he tricked Cathy into inviting us both for dinner. By the time we got through with them, they were on the verge of divorce themselves."

"That's not my fault. He shouldn't have lied to her."

"His intentions were the best."

"You know what the road to hell is paved with," she reminded him tartly. "Honesty's more important in a marriage than good intentions—honesty and *faithfulness*."

His broad chest rose in a plaintive sigh. "I've been faithful, Ivy."

"I don't want to hear this again." She started to rise and he put out a hand to stop her. Steeling herself, she waited for yet another explanation she wouldn't believe.

"I love you," he said.

Of all the things he might have said, this was the one she couldn't resist. She loved him, too, dammit. But still she said stubbornly, "I saw you with my own eyes."

"No, you didn't. Admit it—the whole thing could have happened exactly the way I said it did."

"And maybe Scarlett really *did* get Rhett back, but I doubt it." She shook her head emphatically. "I don't even know why I was so surprised. The romance went out of our marriage long ago."

He leaned forward, his knees nearly touching hers. "Why would you say such a thing? What did I ever do to—"

"It's more what you didn't do." She scooted back an inch or so, putting needed space between them. "Admit it, Jack. We were in a rut, our marriage was in a rut."

"The hell it was!"

"The thrill was gone. I wasn't enough to satisfy you anymore."

"What gave you that idea?" he demanded, looking both angry and confused.

"You did. Okay, to be perfectly honest, I'm as guilty—*almost* as guilty as you are."

"Guilty of what?" He looked completely befuddled. "I swear, Ivy, I don't know what you're talking about."

"My point exactly. We're not on the same wavelength anymore. You lead your life, I lead mine. We get together once in a while, usually in bed, and that's about it."

A muscle twitched in his rigid jaw. "No."

"When's the last time you sent me flowers?"

"I've been sending you roses every day of this cruise—or I damned well should have been."

"Oh, Jack! Flowers don't count when you're just trying to get out of trouble. I mean—well, for example, do you remember when we first met?"

"Sure I do."

"You sent me flowers all the time, back then. And you brought me presents and wined and dined me. Even after we got married, we'd spend hours just . . . just holding hands and staring into each other's eyes." She laughed bitterly. "Now we just hit the sack and get on to more important things."

He looked stricken. "Nothing's more important to me than you are, Ivy. Okay, maybe I'm not as romantic as I used to be—"

"—when you were trying to get me into bed."

"—and maybe I've fallen into a few bad habits—"

"Bad habits! I'd say sleeping with other women is a little bit more than a bad habit."

"Other *women?*" He looked appalled. "You mean you think there's been more than one?"

"Aha! Then you admit there's been *at least* one?"

"I don't admit a damn thing." His face was a study in frustration. "I didn't sleep with Tiffani, I swear to God, I didn't. If I'm guilty of anything, it's simple bad judgment."

"Which means what, exactly?"

"I knew she was trying to hit on me." The words seemed to come with painful effort. "I guess I was flattered. But I didn't know she'd follow me home, and I sure as hell didn't know she'd crawl into our bed the minute my back was turned."

She wanted to believe him. More than anything in the world, she wanted to believe him. "J-Jack—" She swallowed hard and forced herself to hold his pleading gaze. "Did you at least kiss her?" she asked, thinking of Florida.

His face seemed to freeze, and then he groaned. "Ah, Ivy..."

"Tell the truth, Jack," she whispered.

She could actually see the struggle going on beneath his frozen surface. Finally, with an effort so enormous she could feel it, he nodded.

And muttered a strangled "Yes!" before adding quickly, "But it was more a case of her kissing me. It didn't mean anything, Ivy, I swear it."

The thought of Jack kissing another woman made her blood run cold, despite memories of a certain gentleman who'd made a few moves of his own. She'd rationalized her response to Bart Van Horn, even patting herself on the back for resisting temptation in the form of a kiss.

Looking at Jack, a sudden thought occurred to her: he might be telling the truth. But even if he weren't, *There but for the grace of God go I.*

"Maybe..." She looked into his earnest brown eyes, and a surge of love overwhelmed her. "Maybe I could overlook a kiss, if that's all it was."

"Cross my heart and hope to die." Quick hope flared in his face, and he traced a big X over his chest. "Ivy, I love you. I've never loved anyone else."

"Jack, oh, Jack, I—"

As if of one mind, they melted into each other's arms. With a groan that sounded like relief, Jack kissed first one corner of her mouth, then the other.

"I've missed you," he murmured. "You don't know how much."

"Don't I?" Her laugh was throaty, sexy. "This hasn't been easy for me, either. But if you tell me you didn't make love to Wal-Mart—"

"Yeah, Wal-Mart." He smoothed his hands over her shoulders, working them beneath the straps of her swimsuit.

"—then I've got to believe you. But if you ever so much as look at another woman—"

"Never did, never will."

He eased her down on the blanket, onto her back, covering her mouth with his exactly as she knew he would. A shiver ran through her, a shiver of anticipation she hadn't felt in a very long time. She opened her mouth to him, and he accepted the invitation; she parted her thighs and he slipped one knee between them, pressing against her intimately.

She couldn't believe she was about to let him make love to her right here on the beach. On the other hand she didn't believe anything in the world could stop them with the fever rising to match the temperature.

Unfortunately she was wrong.

She hadn't taken Bart into consideration.

11

JACK STOPPED KISSING her and lifted his head to look down the beach. What he saw brought a torrent of swearwords pouring from his mouth. Ivy stirred beneath him, her arms tightening possessively around his waist.

"What is it?" she murmured, blinking as if she'd just been pulled out of deep, deep sleep.

For Jack, what Bart Van Jerk had interrupted was closer to a dream than simple slumber. He had spent untold hours imagining this very situation, both before and after his fall from grace. It seemed as if she'd been in Florida for a month of Sundays, and then her return had precipitated a disaster of untold magnitude.

All he'd had, for a very long time, were dreams—hot, passionate dreams of having Ivy on a tropical island, wrestling around on a sugar-sand beach, driving them both so crazy with love that they didn't care about anything except each other and—

"I'll kill the son of a bitch," Jack growled deep in his throat. It sounded like a sacred promise.

"Who? What—is that *Bart?*" Ivy yanked at the top of her swimsuit, which Jack had succeeded in lowering to her waist. Watching those luscious breasts disappear from view made him even madder than he already was, which was plenty.

He had no choice but to roll over and let her sit up, which she quickly did. The flush on her cheeks came from inside, not from the tropical sun, and it reminded Jack anew of what he was missing. Five more minutes and they'd have been *together* again in every sense of the word.

Bart strolled up, a nasty smile on his face. He'd approached from around a curve in the beach, not through the trees, which explained why Mitchell hadn't headed him off at the pass.

Bart's opening gambit was a glib, "Lovely day to enjoy the beach."

"Yeah, lovely," Jack mocked. He slipped his arm around Ivy's waist and glared at this interloper.

She didn't protest his touch. "What are you doing here, Bart?" she asked breathlessly.

Bart's smile didn't slip. "Looking for you, actually. It appears I may have found you a tad too late."

"Too late for what?" Jack demanded.

Bart shrugged. "I'd say that at this point it doesn't much matter. If Ivy's willing to overlook your indiscretions, who am I to quibble?"

"Yeah, who indeed?"

"What indiscretions?" Ivy frowned. "Honestly, Bart, you don't know anything about this."

"Maybe not," he agreed, the picture of perversion. "I *do* know that a lot of women wouldn't be as forgiving as you are." He started to turn away. "Too each his own."

An icy finger of fear raked Jack's exposed backbone. "Right. See you around, then."

Bart took the hint and a step back the way he'd come.

"*Just* a minute." Ivy's brow wrinkled. "Lots of women wouldn't forgive what?"

"Why—" How the hell could a land developer look that innocent without collapsing into helpless laughter? "I'm talking about Rusti, of course."

"Rusti!" Jack and Ivy repeated in unison, exchanging startled glances. She added, "What about Rusti?"

Bart took another step back, holding up his hands in a placating gesture. "Look, this is your business. If it's okay with you, it's okay with me."

"*What are you talking about?*" Ivy demanded. "I haven't got a clue!"

"Obviously you do, but if you want to play dumb—"

His words twisted like a knife in Jack's gut. Ivy's mother had played dumb and Ivy had sworn she'd never take that path, no matter what. "Ivy," he said thickly, his grip on her tightening, "we don't have to listen to this."

"I want to hear what he has to say." She sat up straighter. "What is it you think I know, Bart?"

"I don't want to rub your nose in anything. I respect you too much for that." The face Bart turned on Jack would have stopped boiling lava in its course. "If you're willing to forget where he slept last night, it's nothing to me."

"Where he—?" Ivy frowned. "He's been sleeping with the crew. Desmond told me."

Good old Desmond, Jack thought. So that explained her change of heart. "That's right," he said quickly. "Ivy, why don't we find us a spot with a little more privacy?" He tried to hustle her to her feet, but she wasn't buying.

She looked at Bart coldly. "Not until he apologizes."

"I have nothing to apologize for," Bart said with soft malice. "I said, last night. Where did your husband sleep *last night?*"

And then Jack knew; Bart had seen him sneaking into Rusti's room. Jack wasn't a particularly violent man, but at that precise moment he was seriously contemplating murder.

Ivy looked confused. "He slept with the crew. Right, Jack? Tell him that you never..." Her voice trailed off and she stared at him in horror.

The trapdoor had sprung wide and quicksand sucked him under...but not, unfortunately, fast enough to keep him from crying out, "It isn't what you're thinking, Ivy. I can explain!"

This was not what she wanted to hear.

"I DON'T BELIEVE IT," Mitchell said firmly. He and Ivy were in the limo on their way back to the ship, she slumped in a corner while he tried to soothe her with only limited success.

"He admitted it," she said in a shaky voice. "And you know what he had the nerve to say? *'I can explain!'* That's the same thing he said when I found him with that other bimbo!

"Maybe he *can* explain."

"Give it up, Mitchell." She glared at him, feeling tears tremble on her lashes and hating her own weakness. "Anything can be explained if you're already grasping at straws. Murder can be explained, for heaven's sake—*explained,* but not *justified.* Some women will swallow their pride and believe anything. My mother—'' She turned her head sharply, staring through the window at the verdant landscape.

She'd made such a fool of herself. In another five minutes Bart would have been too late. As humiliated as she felt now, how would she have felt then? She ought to *thank* him for what he'd done.

''Bart's a troublemaker,'' Mitchell said suddenly. ''He did this deliberately. He's after you, you know.''

''I *do* know, but what he said was true. Jack didn't even try to deny it. All he wanted was to explain, to justify, to—to cop a plea.''

''Still, you can't trust a man who'd insinuate himself into a situation like this.''

''Who said anything about trust? I've never trusted Bart and I never will.'' Ivy turned suddenly and grabbed Mitchell's hands. ''It's between Jack and me, and this time it's really over. I was weakening—okay, I was ready to take him back and forgive everything. Now I realize what a horrible mistake that would have been.''

Mitchell looked alarmed. ''I hope this doesn't—''

''It does,'' she said quickly. ''I'm going through with my original plan.''

Mitchell groaned. ''Surely you don't mean—''

''Exactly. I'm going to sleep with another man before this cruise is over.''

''If you do that, your *marriage* will be over,'' Mitchell argued.

''Because Jack would never forgive me? I'm supposed to forgive *him,* but he'll never forgive me?''

"No, Ivy. Because you'll never forgive yourself."

She caught her breath. "You're wrong," she said without measurable conviction. "Anything he can do, I can do with ten times the justification."

"Lord, you young people make things tough on yourselves. Think long and hard, Ivy. Are you absolutely sure that's what you want?"

"I'm absolutely sure it's *not* what I want, but I have no choice."

"We always have choices."

"You tried, Mitchell. Now it's time to give it up, okay?"

He pressed her no further, for which she was grateful. By the time they reached the cruise ship, she'd managed to convince herself that she'd regained her equilibrium.

She labored under that misapprehension right up until she ran into Bart in the passageway outside her stateroom.

"Can I come in?" Bart asked, glancing around her at the half-open door.

"That's not a good idea," she hedged. "I'll see you later at dinner."

"Now, Ivy."

He reached across her shoulder and pressed the door wider, not in a threatening way but determinedly nonetheless. Shrugging, she let him follow her inside.

Her cabin was immaculate, bed made, fresh flowers on the bedside table beside a bucket of fresh ice and a pitcher of tea. How Desmond knew when she'd be returning, she couldn't imagine.

Desmond!

But she couldn't call him and ask questions with Bart hovering over her.

"Would you like a glass of tea?" she said, stalling.

"No, thanks. I'm here for conversation, not refreshments." Without invitation, he sat on the foot of the bed. "I guess you've figured out that it was no accident, me finding you and Jack on the beach."

"It had occurred to me." She fixed herself a glass of iced tea and sat on the bench against the wall, well away from him.

"I'm sure it hurt you to hear the truth that way. I thought you needed to know."

"Probably, but it's like taking bitter medicine—you may need it and it may save your life in the long run, but that still doesn't mean you enjoy it at the time."

He nodded. "I really did regret hurting you."

"I believe you," she said shortly. "Is that all?"

"No." A slight smile curved his mouth. "I know what you're up to."

"What I'm—?" She felt hot blood rush into her cheeks. He couldn't! Not really...

He leaned forward and spoke with complete assurance. "If you're going to get even with Jack by sleeping with another man, why not me?"

"I—what—good grief!" She stumbled around, trying to find words to deflect the truth. She finally settled on "What are you talking about? And how did you find out?"

Being an intelligent man, he ignored the first question and answered the second. "I eavesdropped." He gave a self-deprecating little laugh.

"You eavesdropped?"

He nodded. "On Jack and Mitchell. They were talking in a booth in the Sweetheart Lounge and I . . . sort of slipped into the booth behind them."

She felt sick to her stomach. "They were discussing *me?*"

"Actually, Jack was doing most of the talking. He seemed quite shocked when Mitchell admitted knowing what you planned to do. I'm a little shocked myself—not that your husband doesn't deserve it, you understand."

This was too humiliating! "I don't want to talk to you about it," she said, and her voice cracked. "You'd better go now." *You've done quite enough to me for one day!*

"All right." He rose. "I only have one question."

"And that is?" Anything to get rid of him.

"I understand perfectly why you have to do this."

"That's not a question."

"This is the question." He paused, obviously for dramatic effect. *"If not me, who?"*

Who, indeed?

She watched him leave, gave it five minutes and then opened the door. Sticking her head into the hall, she saw Desmond approaching.

She gestured frantically. He looked around to see if she meant him, then approached with a big smile.

"How may I serve you, m'lady?"

"You can answer a question."

He frowned. "I will try, m'lady."

She took a deep breath meant to steady her skittering heart. "Desmond, where did Jack—where did my husband sleep last night? I mean, did he sleep in the crew's quarters or did he go . . . somewhere else?"

Desmond's eyes widened. "Ohhh, milady, he had to move. We picked up another waiter in Martinique and he took your husband's bunk. Poor ol' Jack, I don't know where he went then. I was hopin'—" His dark glance darted past her to the door and he shrugged. "We all been thinkin' you and your mister make up."

Her last drop of hope evaporated. "I see." She bit her lip. "Thank you for telling me. And for the ice and the tea."

"It's nothin', m'lady." He gave her a slight bow. "Anything to make you happy."

He walked away jauntily, whistling under his breath and looking well pleased with life. Ivy, not pleased with much of anything and a long way from happy, went back inside her cabin and had herself a good cry.

AT DINNER that night, Ivy was the life of the party, small party though it was. She'd dressed carefully, pulling out all the stops to look glamorous and care-free and happy.

She wore her new blue dress, the one that brought out the color in her eyes, and she'd made her face up with special care. No way would she let Jack see how miserable he'd made her. No way would she let Bart see the same thing.

All her planning went for naught when Jack failed to appear for the meal. That really ticked her off. It was as if he'd taken her rejection on the beach as final.

Which of course it was, she hastily assured herself. She was through with Jack Conrad forever. But not for a moment had she imagined Jack would accept that. She found the possibility that he had completely depressing.

How did you get even with someone who no longer cared?

As if intent on playing along with her manic gaiety, Mitchell ordered a bottle of champagne. Holding up his crystal flute, he smiled at his table companions.

"Anyone care to make a toast?"

Ivy hesitated, clinging to her smile. "To new beginnings," she said.

Mitchell frowned. "To old times," he offered.

Bart leaned forward. "If not me, who?" He grinned broadly.

Ivy laughed. "You're incorrigible," she said, but drank just the same. She was feeling reckless. Maybe Bart had something there.

FOR THE NEXT two days Ivy threw herself into every activity going. She exercised, took line-dancing lessons, entered—and lost—a Ping-Pong tournament with Bart, learned to play shuffleboard and hated it, and saw every show and every lounge act the ship offered. She did all this with two of her three musketeers at her heels.

The only thing she *didn't* do was have fun.

Which was Jack's fault, naturally. Since they'd been interrupted on the beach, he'd avoided her entirely. She'd seen him a time or two at a distance, but he'd always disappeared before she could get close enough to—to what? She'd not been trying to confront him, she'd simply kept going about her business.

Always, she kept looking...looking for someone with whom to commit hanky-panky. By Friday, she thought she'd met every unmarried guy on this ship, and she'd found them all wanting.

This one was a computer nerd, that one an engineering geek, another was a make-out artist who came on way too strong. Also unsuitable were the farmer from Kansas—she'd end up breaking his heart—the drugstore cowboy from Texas and the nuclear physicist from California.

In a panic, she realized she wasn't getting anywhere. The cruise would end in San Juan, Puerto Rico, at eight o'clock Sunday morning. This was Saturday—Valentine's Day, her seventh anniversary—and all she had left to work with was the big masquerade party tonight.

If something didn't happen...if lightning didn't strike...she didn't know what she'd do.

At that moment Bart leaned over and whispered in her ear: "If not me, who?"

His warm chuckle made her shiver. Nevertheless, he'd stated her problem succinctly.

RUSTI CHARGED into her stateroom and, at the sight of Jack, stopped short.

"Jeez!" she exclaimed. "Don't you ever go out anymore?"

Lying on the spare bed with a stack of magazines and paperback books at his side, Jack shrugged with his eyebrows. "Don't see much point to it," he said, sounding pitiful.

Rusti ripped open a drawer and extracted a clean T-shirt. "I see your wife all over the ship. She sure is having a better time than you are."

Jack frowned. "What's that supposed to mean?"

Rusti tugged off her T-shirt and slipped into the fresh one, not in the least embarrassed to be seen in her bra by her guest. "You know. Abbott and Costello are always tagging along."

"Oh, them." Jack relaxed a bit. "As long as it's a threesome I don't have anything to worry about—I don't think."

Rusti grabbed a comb and ran it through her red hair. "Ivy sure seems determined to have fun. She's almost...manic about it."

Jack sighed. "She's trying to get over me."

"While you sit in here on your butt and let her?" She looked skeptical.

"Absence makes the heart grow fonder."

"Out of sight, out of mind. Does Ivy know about...?" She wiggled her fingers to indicate their current sleeping arrangements.

"Yeah, she does."

Rusti scowled. "How'd she find out?"

"Bart Van Horny told her."

"Of all the nerve! Maybe I should set him straight myself." Rusti drew herself up, the picture of well-developed outrage. "And she believed him instead of you?"

"She believed us both."

"You told her the truth? Jack, you're nuts! I'd have backed you up, whatever you'd said."

"I figured, but I've never lied to her. I don't want to start now."

She gave him a look filled with disbelief. "Even if it means the end of your marriage? I hate to tell you this, Jack, but if you can't melt her heart on a Caribbean cruise, it's all over but the shouting."

"Yeah, I know. That's why I've been layin' low, trying to give her time to cool down before I make my big move."

"Whatever you've got in mind, it better be damn big. And I sure do hope it works, because you're running out of time." She headed back toward the door. "I've got a dance class to put on, babe." She hesitated, casting a speculative glance over one shoulder. "You plan on goin' to the masquerade ball tonight?"

"Oh, yes," Jack said softly. "Definitely. I've got my costume and everything."

"If I don't see you before that, have a good time."

"Thanks." He planned to. He planned to have a *great* time. He'd picked out his costume with great times in mind.

If his wife was looking for someone with whom to be indiscreet, she'd find a willing conspirator behind the mask of Zorro.

Olé!

12

THE GRAND BALLROOM of the *Inamorata II* was grand indeed. Three stories high, it soared upward in splendid array, its majestic height accented by a multitude of tiny white lights that reminded Ivy of fireflies. Crystal fixtures and marble floors glowed beneath the dramatic lighting, emphasizing the opulence of the scene.

Exiting from the glass elevator on the arm of Julius Caesar, Ivy-Scheherazade paused to look around with anticipation mixed with a soupçon of trepidation.

Wait until Jack saw her in this getup, she thought. He was going to have a *fit*.

For Scheherazade's costume was a fantasy of diaphanous veils and a king's ransom in bogus jewels—from the tip of her chiffon-draped, black-wigged head to the toes of her bejeweled sandals.

Between those two points she wore something that looked like a golden bra and a gold-encrusted band around her hips that supported the wafting veils of what could laughingly be called her skirt.

Faux jewels adorned every part of her: fingers, wrists, ankles and throat, even a particularly large and patently phony ruby glued into her exposed belly button.

She'd never worn anything so outrageous in her life—and she loved it. She felt wicked and daring and, of course, she had just cause.

Across the marble floor swirled a motley assortment of revelers: cowboys, *señoritas,* kings and jesters, to mention but a few. The costume du jour, though, was Zorro; there were at least a half-dozen masked men in black.

Mitchell wasn't one of them. He looked absolutely imperial in his white toga with royal purple and gold embroidery. He held the flowing drape with regal ease across one muscular arm, as if he'd done this in some other life. A golden crown of laurel leaves rested on his noble brow.

Damn, the man was good-looking! It was almost a shame he'd become such a good friend.

He leaned close in order to be heard over the efforts of a band. "Shall we find a table while we still can?"

She nodded. "I think over there—"

A toreador bowed low. "May I have this dance, Cleopatra?"

"I'm not Cleopatra, I'm Scheherazade, and—"

He swept her into his arms and whirled her away, so she finished what had begun as a polite disclaimer with "—I'd be delighted."

He guided her across the floor with more enthusiasm than skill. "Heck of a party," he shouted over the racket.

She recognized the voice: the computer nerd. "I just got here," she shouted back. "I haven't had time to find out."

He tugged her closer. "I knew you the minute I saw you."

"How? I'm disguised, or hadn't you noticed?" She strove to keep her distance, which was pretty much an exercise in futility.

He guffawed. "I'd never forget a bod like yours." He leered. "Saw you at the pool the other day and said to myself, I said, there's a woman I'd like to get to know a whole lot—"

"Mind *eef* I cut in, *señor?*"

One of the many Zorros snatched her away without missing a beat. Despite his abominable attempt at a Spanish accent, he was a far better dancer than a linguist.

"You look great, *señorita.*"

"Bart? Is that you under the black mask?"

"Damn!" But it was said in a good-natured way. "The accent didn't fool you?"

She laughed. "For about two seconds. If you'd kept your mouth shut, you'd have been home-free."

His grip tightened. "Don't I just wish. I—"

"May I cut in?"

A cowboy stood there, hat pushed back to reveal curly hair, and a bandanna tied over his face bandit-style and a half mask concealing his eyes.

Jack? She caught her breath. Before she could respond, he snatched her into his arms and whirled her away. When she finally got her bearings, she glared at him.

"What do you think you're doing?" she demanded. "You know I don't want to dance with you or even *see* you."

"Gosh, what'd I do?" asked a plaintive, if decidedly nasal, voice. "I didn't mean anything by it. I've been admiring you from afar, is all. It was all in fun, honest."

Who *was* this guy? Feeling foolish, Ivy apologized effusively. "I thought you were someone else," she concluded. "With all the masks and everything—"

"No problem," her partner said in a voice she now recognized as belonging to the Texan she'd met a few days ago. But he continued to look at her askance and seemed less than reluctant to retreat when the dance ended. In fact, he left her standing on the dance floor in his haste to escape.

Crossing to join Mitchell at a table, Ivy scolded herself with every step. She was getting jumpy, that's what it was; she saw Jack lurking behind every mask. Shoot, he probably wasn't even here. If he was, he wouldn't have the gall to confront her.

Not after what he'd done.

Which wasn't half of what she'd been ready to *let* him do, but that was beside the point. Yep, she owed Bart for saving her from that final humiliation.

MITCHELL AND IVY dined from the sumptuous buffet table with its ice carvings of Cupids and unicorns, they danced when they could find room to wedge themselves onto the floor and when some other masked man wasn't sweeping Ivy away. After a while, she began to tire of the attention her costume solicited, even to the point of thinking longingly of Little Mary Sunshine.

Time and again she suspected some mystery man holding her in his arms of being Jack, and time and again she was proven wrong. Then a movie-perfect sheikh bowed before her and she knew.

This was Jack. Some things you just couldn't fake. She danced with him decorously, neither of them saying a word until the dance ended. When he escorted her back to her table, she reached up to sweep aside his burnoose to reveal—

Kevin.

Jill's Kevin, who laughed delightedly.

"Fool you?" he asked, rearranging everything to mask his face again. "Jill said I would."

"Jill," Ivy said on a sigh, "was right."

"Would you care to join us for a drink?" he asked, glancing at Mitchell. "We're right over there." He pointed to Little Mary Sunshine, waving enthusiastically from a table across the way.

Mitchell glanced at Ivy, catching her almost imperceptible negative motion. "Perhaps later," he said, "after the unmasking."

"That'll be swell," Kevin agreed. "We'll find you after the masks come off."

Ivy sat down, watching him thread his way back to his own table. "I'm really getting edgy," she confessed. "I'd have sworn that was Jack." She eyed Mitchell suspiciously. "You haven't seen him here tonight, have you?"

"No. But would it be so bad if—"

"Don't talk—dance."

And so they did, and then Ivy danced with a beach-boy and another Zorro and a convict in a striped suit and a rock 'n' roller in a leather jacket and another Zorro. Safe behind her many veils, she flirted and laughed and enjoyed herself . . . mostly. But she also kept watching for Jack, wondering if he were here watching her, wondering if he felt jealous and left out.

She certainly hoped so.

A sudden shower of balloons and confetti wafted down on the dancers, and she stumbled in surprise. "What's going on?" she asked her partner, who hadn't said a word since he'd taken her into his arms.

"Eet iz time for ze unmasking," he said in a husky whisper made laughable by the phony accent.

Bart, she realized. "That accent is an affront to an entire country," she informed him. "I know who you are so why don't you drop the—"

He effectively cut off her words by hauling her into his arms. Around them, lights flashed on and off, balloons and confetti fell unabated, and a voice boomed over the loudspeaker.

"Time to reveal all, ladies and gentlemen. Take off those masks and greet your partner with a great big Valentine's kiss—"

Ivy's partner reached for the jeweled pin that fastened a veil over the lower part of her face. The wisp of chiffon floated away and she stared up at him—or tried to, for confetti made her blink and close her eyes.

But she felt his hands curve around the sides of her face, tilting it up. And then warm lips touched first one corner of her mouth, then the other, before taking it in a kiss of drugging depth and sweetness—

And she knew; *this was Jack.* Jack, good old predictable Jack. He might confuse her with his dancing and his voice, but he'd never confuse her with his kiss.

And she'd tell him so, too, just as soon as...as soon as... With a sigh she melted against him, lifting her arms to encircle his neck. She'd missed him so damn much that she would even overlook his predictability... for a little while, anyway.

They fit together with the ease of long practice, as if they'd been made for each other. Dimly she felt him slide one hand across the bare skin of her rib cage and down to cover the curve of her hip, dragging her closer still.

The familiarity of his kiss in no way lessened its power, she discovered. She had missed him so very much—but was she willing to overlook all his many transgressions? Was she indeed her mother's daughter?

He trailed little nibbling kisses across her cheek to her ear. "Weel you join me for a leetle stroll around the deck, *señorita?*" he asked in that husky whisper. "Een the moonlight, we can make *bello* music together—"

"Damn you, Jack!" Ivy pushed out of his arms and struck him a sharp rap on the shoulder with her fist. "You've got to be the biggest jerk ever to sail the seven seas."

He rubbed the shoulder she'd struck. His black fabric Zorro mask had been pushed up just enough to allow him to kiss her, but now he shoved it down around his throat. He grimaced. "How'd you know it was me?"

"How did I—?" Whirling, she stomped away from him, weaving her way through couples embracing, kissing. It was disgusting.

He caught up with her and swung her around. "No, seriously. How'd you know it was me when there are a dozen Zorros here?"

"I knew it was you because I'm not an idiot!" She jerked free and stalked on toward her table. Mitchell waited for her there, an anxious expression on his face.

Jack followed. "I never suggested you were an idiot," he protested. "But I'd have sworn you thought I was someone else."

"Right up until you kissed me."

Jack's frown lifted. "Damn, that's great. It's the old magic, Ivy. Don't deny it, honey—just you and me."

She stared at him, hands on her hips. "Have you lost your mind? That's not it at all!"

He looked wounded. "You mean you didn't feel that kiss all the way down to your toes?"

Wild horses couldn't have pulled that admission from her. "I *mean*, you've kissed me exactly the same way for years. I could pick your kiss out of a million because it's so... so *predictable.*"

"Predictable?" Old Zorro looked mystified, and maybe a little insulted.

"Predictable!" Stepping up to him, she bracketed his lean cheeks with her hands. "First you kiss the right corner of my mouth—"

This she proceeded to do.

"Then you kiss the other corner of my mouth—"

Again, she demonstrated.

"Then you kiss me square-on."

She did, quick and hard.

"And then you grab—well, never mind what you grab, we're in polite company." She darted an apologetic glance at Mitchell, who watched as if mesmerized.

She dropped her arms to her sides and took a step away from Jack. "I'm tired of it, Jack. I'm tired of you operating on remote control. Even if we didn't have that . . . *other* problem, which of course we do, I still couldn't give us better than a fifty-fifty chance of making it together."

He looked completely stunned. "I had no idea you felt this way. Why didn't you say something?"

"I did! Why do you think I kept agitating for this cruise? I thought we could put a little romance back into our marriage."

"And we can! There's still time." He tried to take her into his arms.

She avoided his embrace. "The cruise ends tomorrow. Instead of making things better, it's made things worse—lots worse. Now I not only have your Texas sweetie to get over, there's your cruise ship sweetie as well."

Jack's shock seemed to be passing and a new, harder glint appeared in his eyes. "I've never been unfaithful to you, Ivy. I love you as much now as when we were first married."

"Which was seven years ago today—actually yesterday, since it's past midnight. Seven years, Jack. That's a long time. You've got the seven-year itch and you found somebody else to scratch it!"

"Is that what you really think?"

"It's what I know."

"If you're that sure, maybe we *don't* have anything to talk about."

Spinning around on the balls of his feet, he took a determined step and Ivy held her breath. Was this really it, then? Was their marriage truly over?

He whirled back to face her. "What about you?" he snarled.

"Me?" That caught her by surprise.

"Yeah, you. And that land raper—"

"Developer!"

"—jerk from Florida?"

"There's nothing between me and Bart and you know it."

"How do I know it?"

"Because I say so!" Ooops, that was weak. "Because you've got no evidence to the contrary," she amended.

"He's spent time in your cabin. Maybe that's proof enough."

"Don't be ridiculous."

"He's warm for your form." His critical glance swept over her revealing costume. "Him and half the men here."

"Why, Jackie Conrad," she purred, pleased with this turn of events, "don't tell me you're jealous."

"Do I have reason to be?"

"Of course not."

"Van Horn never tried to kiss you?"

She lifted her chin. "That's insulting. I'm not going to answer it."

"He *did* kiss you."

"I didn't say that, but what if he did? Macy—"

"Tiffani!"

"—kissed you, you admitted it."

He jerked his chin toward the still-crowded dance floor. "When we were dancing, you thought I was Van Horn at first."

"What if I did?"

"You shouldn't have let me dance that close to you, that's what. It wasn't...decent for a married woman. And then you let me kiss you."

"And I knew it was you. I already told you that. Nothing's changed, Jack, and apparently nothing ever will. We're *boring* together. I'll bet I'm as predictable to you as you are to me."

He pulled himself up with stiff indignation. "You are—" It was as if he'd planned to add a decisive *not* and couldn't pull it off. "I love you enough that I'm willing to settle for what the hell ever we've got."

"We've got nothing."

"Then let's start over—start from scratch, if we have to."

"Did you sleep with either of those women?"

"No. Did you sleep with Van Horny?"

"*No!* Not yet, anyway."

"I'll believe you if you'll believe me."

His offer hung in the air between them...but in the final analysis, she couldn't buy it.

She bit her lip and looked away. "I'm still morally superior to you, and that makes it impossible for me to respect you. I can't live with a man I don't respect."

Love him, maybe; not respect him or live with him.

For a long moment he just looked at her. Then he said, "I guess you really are pure as the driven snow, in thought as well as deed."

Ivy flashed back on a hot Florida night and a handsome man putting the moves on her. It was an effort to hold herself still before her husband's seeking gaze. "I never said I was a saint," she muttered.

"Maybe not, but you *are* morally superior. I lusted in my heart, and then only a little. Hell, Ivy, even one of our former presidents confessed to that much. I'm only human."

"Are you saying I'm not?"

He shrugged. "If you've never even been tempted, I'd say you're either not human or you're already dead and don't know it. I've leveled with you about what happened. If that's enough to end our marriage, I guess there's nothing more I can do about it."

He gave her the saddest look she'd ever seen. "I love you," he said, "but if you sleep with another man, it's all over but the shouting."

Turning, he walked away, leaving her to wonder if those long strides were carrying him out of her life forever.

IVY SAT at the table with Mitchell, swilling champagne and growing more angry by the moment.

"How dare he issue ultimatums?" she demanded for the umpteenth time. "Who does he think he is?" She reached for the wine bottle.

Mitchell covered her hand with his to discourage a refill. "He's hurt, Ivy, just as you are."

"He started it." She glared at him.

"Maybe, but there's no proof he slept with that woman in Dallas. The only proof we have is that she was after him." Mitchell's eyes narrowed thoughtfully. "Much as Bart Van Horn is after you. Ivy, what happened in Florida?"

"Nothing." She looked away. "Okay, he...made a few moves. Which I valiantly resisted, unlike some people I could name."

"Were you tempted?"

She drew a deep, disgusted breath, then heard herself saying, "So what if I was? Nothing happened!"

"That's what Jack says."

"Only *I'm* telling the truth."

"He could be, too."

"Maybe, but what about Rusti? He's still sleeping with her, isn't he?"

"He's still sleeping in her room. There's a difference. You threw him out of his room so he's got to sleep somewhere."

"Yeah, right."

"Ivy, listen to me." He caught her hands in his and stared into her eyes. "Rusti's engaged."

"My God! Jack isn't even divorced yet!"

Mitchell looked annoyed. "To a man she met on a cruise ship last year. He surprised her in Barbados and gave her a ring. She's quitting as soon as the ship docks in San Juan."

"Jack told you this?"

"Rusti told me this. She wanted me to tell you that there's nothing going on between her and Jack but friendship. She'd have told you yourself, but she didn't think you'd listen to her."

"She thought right. Even if I did, that still leaves the other one to be explained."

Mitchell smiled. "Ivy, if you can explain Bart, you can certainly understand about Gimbel."

"Macy. And I can't." She gritted her teeth so hard they ached. "I'm going to do what I came on this cruise to do." She stood up abruptly.

He looked alarmed. "Where do you think you're going?"

She smiled at him with champagne-induced cunning. "To look for Bart," she said. "If I've got the name, I may as well have the game."

13

THE MINUTE THE THOUGHT occurred to her, she knew she had to run with it.

She'd sleep with Mitchell Kerr.

It was the only solution; now all she had to do was convince him of that. He'd all but become Jack's champion, for heaven's sake. That left her with only one alternative.

She'd trick him into it.

Mitchell was glaring at her. "Don't start that again, Ivy." His face had gone positively white.

"Why, whatever do you mean?" she asked, knowing perfectly well.

"That lecherous dog Van Horn's been hounding you since this ill-fated cruise began. I refuse to believe you'd allow it to go any further."

She let out her breath on a long, low note redolent of regret. "What else can I do?"

"Anything but that."

"All right, Mitchell."

He looked surprised, then pleased. "You mean…?"

"I mean I won't go in search of Bart—if you'll sleep with me instead."

The hands holding hers clenched spasmodically. The blue Paul Newman eyes went wide with shock.

"That's...that's out of the question. You don't know what you're asking."

"I do!" When he would have withdrawn his hands, she clung to them. "I've got to do this, Mitchell. You're..." She bit her lip. "You're the least objectionable, by far."

He groaned. "Thanks for that, anyway."

"I don't mean to hurt your feelings," she insisted, "but you know what I'm trying to say. I'm not doing this for fun. In fact, I don't want—" Or *deserve!* "—any fun. I'm doing it to make a point."

"You mean," Mitchell said rather coldly, "to erase your moral superiority where Jack's concerned? To lower yourself to his level, as it were?"

"Well...yes."

"What if you get there and discover that you've lowered yourself right on past his level? That he's told you the truth, but it's too late because you've sold yourself for a...a mess of pottage?"

She raised both brows. "Aren't you mixing similes or something?"

He gave an exasperated grunt. "I'm trying to save you from yourself, and you're making jokes. You don't want to sleep with Bart Van Horn."

"That's right. I want to sleep with you."

"Don't say that again!" He managed to yank his hands away at last. "I'm not made of stone, you know."

"Actually, I didn't. This is the first indication you've given me that you might be flesh and blood."

"Damn, Ivy, in that outfit you could bring a statue to its knees. I'm a grandfather, for the love of Mike! Have a heart!"

"You're kidding!"

"Do I look like I'm kidding? I have a two-year-old grandson."

"Does that mean you've forgotten how to do it?"

"Why you young—!" He bit off the exclamation. "It means I've forgotten more than you'll ever know."

"Prove it."

"I don't have to prove a thing."

My goodness, she thought with satisfaction, *he's getting flustered.* "All right," she agreed, tightening the noose. "Bart it is."

"Bart it *isn't.*" He sucked in a deep, agitated breath, his face taut. Then he held out his hand, wiggling his fingers. "Give me your damned key."

"Do you mean it?"

"What do you want me to do, draw you a picture?"

"Oh, Mitchell, how can I ever thank you?" Digging around in her small evening purse, she extracted her extra plastic key and handed it over. Still afraid he'd change his mind, she added hopefully, "But wouldn't you rather just go to my cabin with me now and get it over with?"

He took her card and turned it over and over in his hand. His gaze bored into her with an intensity that made her shiver. "I've learned a few things in those extra years. One of them is that little girls who play with fire oftentimes get burned."

"I have no intention of being burned," she said with dignity. "I explained all that. This is simply something that must be done."

"Like a root canal."

She lifted her chin. "Something like that."

"That's what *you* think."

She blinked. "What's that supposed to mean?"

He rose and leaned toward her, his hands on the tabletop. She'd never felt intimidated by him, but now she did.

"From here on out," he said, "it's my call."

"Now wait a minute." She stood up, too. "I'm not looking for anything fancy."

"Too late."

"But, Mitchell!" She frowned at him. "I thought you were my friend."

"I am. That's why I'm promising you—"

"It sounds more like a warning."

"*Promising* you a night of unbridled passion, the likes of which you haven't experienced since—" he seemed to cast about for an appropriate comparison "—since your honeymoon."

She took a step back. "You're getting into the spirit of this a bit more than I'd expected."

He held her card key in the air. "Too late to change your mind," he said with a faintly wolfish grin. "If you'll excuse me, I have a few things to take care of before our... assignation."

"All right," she agreed with reluctance, "but don't you dare try to make me enjoy this. Don't you dare, because I won't."

She wouldn't because she was simply trying to save her marriage. Sex without love was just that: sex. She'd do what she had to do but *no way* would she enjoy it.

No way!

IVY WAS, to put it mildly, a nervous wreck. Pacing in the confines of her stateroom, she practiced deep breathing and excuses while she waited for Mitchell.

She couldn't do this; she was sick. She placed a hand experimentally over her silk-covered abdomen and groaned. Tension could make you sick, couldn't it? Tension and guilt and shame...

Pausing before the mirror, she stared at her reflection in the sexy black nightgown that she'd bought way back when she was still a semihappily married woman. What in the world was she doing? This wasn't her! This was some tart named Tiffani—yes, her hated rival's name was Tiffani, not Macy, not Gimbel, not even—cheap as she was—Wal-Mart.

With hands that trembled, Ivy dialed Mitchell's stateroom. The telephone rang and rang and rang, but nobody answered.

He was on his way! Racing into the postage-stamp-size bathroom, Ivy snatched out her heavy terry cloth robe and belted it tightly. Then she stood staring at the door, waiting for that dreaded knock.

Twenty minutes or so later, she realized she had no idea where Mitchell was or when he'd arrive, or even if he was actually coming. With a sigh she sat down on the love seat before the window. Below her the restless sea mirrored her torment.

Gradually the realization of just how wrong this was swamped her. She couldn't go through with it. She'd tell Mitchell so, if he actually showed up, which she was beginning to seriously doubt. In the meantime...

Turning off the lamp, she crawled into bed. Watching moonlight on the water, she fell asleep thinking about how topsy-turvy everything in her world seemed to be at the moment.

"RELA-A-AX..."

She heard the husky admonition as if in a dream. But the electric sensations scampering up and down her spine were no dream, and neither was the heavy pressure of a strong male body against her back, of muscular arms encircling her.

She drifted, not understanding anything except how good it felt...hands massaging her shoulders, lips pressing little kisses on the side of her neck. Like a puppet on a string, she found herself responding instead of thinking.

"Ummmph?" she groaned, snuggling deeper into silky cotton sheets. Still half-asleep she arched her back and sighed.

And remembered.

"Good grief!" She couldn't let Mitchell do this to her...even if it did feel like heaven.

"Shhh..." Again, that calming murmur. Strong hands held her until she stopped struggling. One of his arms slid beneath hers; she felt the warmth of his breath on her ear and shivered, felt the possession of his palm, cupping the undercurve of her breast.

Instinctively she pressed against him, her breast swelling to fill his hand. Her nipple leapt to attention, and he separated his fingers just enough to pinch gently at the pebbled flesh.

And all the while he nibbled on her ear, sending fresh tremors coursing through her. At the flick of his tongue, she tensed; she groaned; she tried to turn toward him but he wouldn't allow it. And then she understood.

It would be his call. His timetable, his dance, and so very different from what she'd become accustomed to in the past several years. He intended to take his own sweet time.

He didn't know she'd decided she couldn't go through with this. She'd tell him so, the very moment she managed to catch her breath.

In the meantime, he explored her body, his hands sliding beneath her silky gown to probe, smooth, examine as carefully as if he could actually see in the pitch-darkness of the cabin.

While she just lay there, marveling at his expertise—in a purely intellectual way, of course. She really *hadn't* felt anything like this since her honeymoon.

And it was all wrong!

Wrong of her to enjoy this man's touch, to want him as desperately as she had wanted Jack on their wedding night; wrong to feel her control shattering into a million tiny shards.

She'd...get hold of herself any minute now, she thought, biting her lip to keep from groaning with delight. Any minute now...

He turned her onto her back and she let him. She was, in fact, unable to make even a token resistance. He slipped her gown from her body and she let him do that, too, then let him use his lips and hands to deal her one exquisite surprise after another. She was flying high, dizzy with sensation.

Still taking his time, he began a slow, sultry slide down her body to her feet, then back up again. With ever-deepening touches and caresses, kisses and nibbles, he kept her gasping. Every place he touched seemed to spring to new life.

Ivy twisted her hands in the sheets to keep from losing control completely. If she hadn't thought she'd die of delight, she would certainly have mentioned to him that she'd changed her mind and had no intention of... what had she no intention of...?

She felt him grow hard and throb against her. A heavy pressure, familiar and yet strangely alien, built in the pit of her stomach. Shocked...enthralled...she still foggily told herself she wouldn't make that final surrender. It simply wasn't right that a man other than Jack could bring her to such a fever pitch of pure, unadulterated desire.

What kind of woman was she, to let this happen when she knew it was wrong?

And then a horrible realization hit her right between the eyes: she was *human* and she'd got herself into a situation she couldn't control. If it could happen to her, it could happen to—

Rational thought shattered; Mitchell was moving her, turning her, lifting and arranging and handling her. Through the mists of her passion, she began to sense his own. He wasn't just using her, he was loving her. The thought terrified her, horrified her...thrilled her.

Stop now! Her conscience screamed at her. *Stop now or never.* Blindly she reached out, intending to shove him away.

Instead, she drew him closer, until he lay upon her, bare skin to bare skin. Her mind might be saying *no-*

no! but her body was shouting *yes-yes!* at the top of its lungs.

Unfortunately for her, Mitchell couldn't read minds. If he could have, he would never have slipped between her thighs—which were, all right, admittedly open to receive him—and joined their bodies with one smooth, silken thrust.

Damn! She'd never gotten around to telling him the whole deal was off....

THEY LAY QUIETLY in the dark, their breathing slowly returning to normal—and at least one of them trying to come to grips with the biggest mistake of her life.

Not that she hadn't enjoyed herself; oh, no, not that at all. She'd enjoyed herself *too* much, which shamed and humiliated her, erasing all claims of moral superiority.

Mitchell had been caught up in the moment, obviously. What was her excuse? She'd cold-bloodedly set out to do this thing, and look at her now.

She shifted in his arms. It was so dark that he was nothing more than a shadow, and she had no idea what he was thinking or feeling about what had happened between them.

"Say something," she begged, pressing her cheek against his chest.

A soft, deep rumble of laughter shook him, and she found herself smiling ruefully in return.

"All right, so I'm funny," she grumbled. "This was my idea so I guess it's up to me to do the talking."

The lazy lethargy left him; she felt his sudden tension where their bodies touched in intimate togetherness. She swallowed hard and forced herself to go on.

"This is wrong," she said in a low voice. "I think you'll agree with me that it should never have happened. Jack—" She'd been about to say, *Jack is the only man I'll ever love, even if you did make me forget that for a few minutes.*

What was the etiquette of lying in bed with one man and discussing another? What would the well-mannered person say? What—

—was Mitchell doing?

Springing out of bed, he bumbled around in the dark, apparently throwing on his clothing.

Ivy sat up in alarm. "Hey, wait a minute! You can't run out on me like this. I'm sorry I hurt your feelings—"

The door slammed behind him and she was talking to herself, not to Mitchell Kerr.

FOR THE REST of the night, Ivy paced around her cabin feeling like the worm on her own hook. It wasn't easy to reconcile what she'd done, for she'd not only committed adultery, she'd had a great time doing it.

Unfortunately the piper must be paid—later, she devoutly hoped. Much later. Eventually she'd tell Jack everything, because she'd have to. Then if he'd forgive her, she'd forgive him. Sadder but wiser, they could enter their eighth year of marriage, leaving the dreaded seven-year itch in the dust.

At least, that's what she hoped, because she knew for a fact that she loved him, no matter what—why else would she feel like this? But if she ran into him too soon, she'd end up confessing everything. She blanched at the thought. And she still had Mitchell to deal with....

A knock on her cabin door brought her bolting to her feet. She cast about wildly for a place to hide, then realized that in a ship's cabin the possibilities were limited.

Neither Jack nor Mitchell stood at her door. She looked at Bart Van Horn and said, "Thank God, it's you."

He blinked. "So who were you expecting?"

"Never mind. What can I do for you?"

"Accept my apologies."

"Your what?"

"I know I made a pest of myself on this cruise. I thought it was for your own good." He shrugged. "But now I'm not so sure."

She waved him inside and closed the door. "What changed your mind?"

He gave her a whimsical smile. "I found out that Rusti Wheeler's engaged to some guy from California. We had breakfast together this morning, and I'm convinced she's never looked at Jack as anything but a friend."

"Then what you said about Jack and Rusti isn't true," Ivy said, feeling relief all the way to her toes.

"Technically it was. He did bunk in her room but I no longer believe they were actually *sleeping together.*"

"And I no longer know what to believe about anything."

He turned back toward the door. "I believe you love your husband, Ivy. Make up with him and get on with the rest of your life—and tell your mother to butt out."

"I may just do that." But she was already wondering: if she'd been wrong about Rusti, might she also be wrong about Tiffani?

Bart stepped into the hall. Before she could get the door closed, Jack barged inside.

Ivy took several running steps backward. Unable to speak, she stared at her husband with shock and horror.

He advanced on her, more intimidating than she'd ever seen him. He scowled, and she noticed that he looked as exhausted as she felt.

His even white teeth gleamed in a snarl. "Okay, Ivy, I've had enough of your games. Are you coming home with me or not?"

"Coming—?" She stared at him, completely baffled.

He advanced another step. "I told you the truth about Macy—"

"Tiffani."

"—and I told you the truth about Rusti."

She licked dry lips. "M-maybe...you did at that."

He blinked. "You mean you believe me?"

"I'm...starting to."

"Then what's the problem? I know you love me. How can you continue to deny it after all that's happened?"

Now was the time to tell him what she'd done; now was the time to confess about last night and throw herself on his mercy. She opened her mouth to say those horrible words, but at that very moment Mitchell appeared behind Jack in the open doorway.

And that dignified individual proceeded to jump up and down and wave frantically, shaking his head *no* and mouthing words she couldn't decipher. What in the—?

And then the light bulb went off over her head and she almost fainted. *It wasn't Mitchell who had come to her in the dark last night, it had been Jack.* She'd committed adultery with her own husband!

With a glad cry, she threw her arms around Jack's neck and hugged him as hard as she could. "Yes!" she cried. "Yes, we can go home together. We can work this out because I love you!"

"That's more like it," he muttered, sounding justifiably annoyed. Suddenly he leaned away from her, although still holding on to her. "You did know that was me last night, didn't you? Mitch told me I'd damned well better love you like you'd never been loved before, and I really put my heart and soul into it. But still..."

Far be it from Ivy Conrad to snatch defeat from the jaws of victory. "Of course I knew it was you," she blustered, trying to look offended at the very idea. "You think I wouldn't know my own husband's love-making?"

Jack frowned. "I didn't think you *did,* until afterward when you called me by name. Why did you say it was all a mistake, Ivy?"

Sputtering, trying to recall exactly what she'd said to him in the aftermath of all that passion, Ivy crossed her fingers behind his back and told as much of the truth as she dared. "I don't even remember what I *did* say, darling. All I know for sure is that I love you, and from now on I'm going to trust you implicitly. Is that good enough?''

''Plenty good.'' He tried to kiss her.

She ducked aside, saw Mitchell beaming with approval just outside the open door and mouthed the words, *Thank you!*

Jack nuzzled her neck. ''You've put me through hell but I guess I deserved it,'' he grumbled. ''I've learned my lesson, though. I'll never take you for granted again, sweetheart. And I swear on a stack of Bibles I'll never look at another woman—or let one look at me.''

''You won't if you know what's good for you,'' she said, clinging to him.

He nibbled on her ear. ''When push came to shove, I knew you wouldn't do it with another man.''

Was there the slightest little bit of doubt in his voice?

''Of course not.'' Grabbing him by the ears, she pulled his face close for a kiss. ''I guess if we can survive the seven-year itch, we can survive anything,'' she said hopefully.

''Damn straight! Mitchell said you had too much pride to give in. He said you all but asked him to send me in his place last night.''

''All but,'' she agreed, thinking she owed Mitchell big-time. She glanced past her husband's shoulder, caught Mitchell's eye and gave him a melting smile brimming with gratitude.

He blew her a kiss, then softly closed the cabin door.

Jack, busy looking at his wife with a salacious gleam in his eyes, didn't notice. ''We've got at least an hour before we have to get off this tub,'' he murmured in a low, sexy purr, ''plenty of time to start scratching that itch. What do you say, Ivy? Shall we get to it?''

As if there were the slightest doubt of her answer....

HE SAID

♥

SHE SAID

Explore the mystery of male/female communication in this extraordinary new book from two of your favorite Harlequin authors.

Jasmine Cresswell and Margaret St. George bring you the exciting story of two romantic adversaries—each from their own point of view!

DEV'S STORY. CATHY'S STORY.
As he sees it. As she sees it.
Both sides of the story!

The heat is definitely on, and these two can't stay out of the kitchen!

Don't miss **HE SAID, SHE SAID.**
Available in July wherever Harlequin books are sold.

HARLEQUIN®

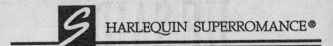

Harlequin® Historical®

If you're a serious fan of historical romance,
then you're in luck!

Harlequin Historicals brings you
stories by bestselling authors, rising new stars
and talented first-timers.

Ruth Langan & Theresa Michaels
Mary McBride & Cheryl St.John
Margaret Moore & Merline Lovelace
Julie Tetel & Nina Beaumont
Susan Amarillas & Ana Seymour
Deborah Simmons & Linda Castle
Cassandra Austin & Emily French
Miranda Jarrett & Suzanne Barclay
DeLoras Scott & Laurie Grant…

You'll never run out of favorites.

Harlequin Historicals…they're too good to miss!

HH-GEN

HARLEQUIN ❖ PRESENTS®

HARLEQUIN PRESENTS
men you won't be able to resist falling in love with...

HARLEQUIN PRESENTS
women who have feelings just like your own...

HARLEQUIN PRESENTS
powerful passion in exotic international settings...

HARLEQUIN PRESENTS
intense, dramatic stories that will keep you turning
to the very last page...

HARLEQUIN PRESENTS
The world's bestselling romance series!

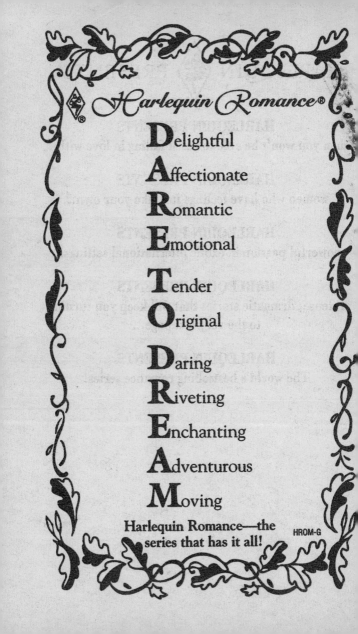

Harlequin Romance®

Delightful
Affectionate
Romantic
Emotional
Tender
Original
Daring
Riveting
Enchanting
Adventurous
Moving

Harlequin Romance—the series that has it all!

HROM-G